Red Kryptonite Curve

Lela Markham

Published by Breakwater Harbor Books

Lela Markham

Text and graphics © 2020 Lela Markham & Lauri Sliney

ISBN # 978-0-9981732-6-9 E-Book edition
ISBN # 978-0-9981732-7-6 Print edition

Lauri Sliney
Aurorawatcher Publications
500 Ketchikan Avenue
Fairbanks, Alaska 99701
lelamarkham@gmail.com

Thanks!

This book is dedicated to my husband Bern, a recovering addict who has taught me to understand what I do not struggle with and not to judge his battles with red kryptonite.

No book is the work of a single individual. The author gets all the glory but standing behind every published writer is a host of support personnel. Peter, Ben and the rest of their friends are borrowed from many struggling young teens I knew over decades as an unchurched teenager, a church youth leader and a mom.

Table of Contents

"One of the problems of being a storyteller is the cultivated ability to extrapolate; in every situation all the *what ifs* come to me."
— **Madeleine L'Engle, The Summer of the Great-Grandmother**

Red Kryptonite Curve

Book 1

What If...Wasn't

Club Class

Peter

Every so often, I dream about walking in on Laren and Sam. I don't remember what I did before that. I'm just in the hallway outside the guestroom when I heard a giggle. Thinking Alyse was teasing me, I opened the door and Sam's head came up from a part of my mother's anatomy that I thought belonged solely to my father. Details have washed over time, but I remember the surge of horror I felt. I knew about sex, I wasn't shocked by seeing it. I just always imagined walking in on my parents and being embarrassed, not this stranger with my mother, which ripped my world apart. I didn't know Sam at the time, but my memory always informs the dream of who he is to me now. Though totally in the wrong doing what he was doing in my father's house, he had the grace to be embarrassed, to grab for a pillow to cover himself and to toss a blanket toward my mother, who has no grace at all. Beautiful Laren Dellinis Wyngate (now Braddock) sat up

1

in all her glorious nudity, her eyes shining with a blue electricity I already knew to fear. Instead of wrapping herself in the blanket and trying to explain to her traumatized 12-year-old son that sometimes adults do incomprehensible things, she reached for me --.

I jolt out of my doze, the lingering sensation of my mother's fingers on my chest following me into waking as if there's no gap of five years. The sleeping pod that seemed cozy a couple of hours ago now becomes an airless coffin that is too short for my body. I fling my long legs out into the aisle, shoving the strangling blanket away. Sweat coats my back and forehead. The plane outside the pod slants ominously. Except for a passenger reading a book across the aisle and a steward hovering in the service niche, Club Class is asleep and neither of them seems to notice the spatial anomaly. I taste vomit at the back of my throat, so pull out my retainer, push to standing and stumble barefoot to the head, shaking, my head pounding. My stomach clenches and turns inside out, dumping its contents into the toilet. It's been more than 24 hours since Collin and I bid a lushy farewell to one another in the hotel bar in London. I can't *still* be hungover. Lacking Tylenol, I wash my face clean of the cloying sweat, but – yeah, I still feel like crap.

When my stomach clenches again, I pull the trigger myself because sometimes it's just better to get the crap out at the front end instead of letting it work its nasty way through to the end. I dry-heave a couple of times and then spew my stomach lining into the toilet. A hot-flash sears through my body.

I'm washing vomit from my mouth when a polite tap sounds on the door and a clipped British voice asks if I'd like my bed turned into a seat and breakfast now or would I prefer to sleep longer. Sleep? That stroll down memory lane had no resemblance to rest. We're still four hours out from JFK. I can't go back into the coffin. Since it appears I'm done puking and my temperature is returning to normal, I opt for breakfast and a book.

"And a bourbon-and-water straight-up."

The steward casts me a skeptical look. British Airways lets you drink at 18, which means I don't technically qualify, but you can buy some excellent ID for a fraction of a trust-fund kid's weekly allowance. Mine says I turned 21 in April. The first swallow settles my stomach and knocks back the headache. I want to drain the glass and order another, but I'm not stupid. Although my fake card worked just fine all across Europe, I know not to push my luck. I am an experienced rule-breaker. I eat fruit, yogurt and a bagel for breakfast while nursing that first drink for an hour, before ordering my next one.

"That must be some great fake ID."

Jorga Persons, America's latest superstar female action lead, sits down in the unoccupied seat in my seating pair and times her comment so the steward is out of earshot. She's gorgeous, though the reality is less awesome than the cinematic version. She's wearing an ordinary pair of black yoga pants and a lime-green tunic with russet embroidery on either side of the vertical slit that doesn't quite invite me to look at her breasts. Like me, she likes to read books while flying. She can't be more than college-aged herself, so I sip my bourbon and branch before I reply to her. Her glossy chocolate-brown hair and sparkling blue eyes belie the muscles I can see in her forearms. She grins at my poker face.

"You are Governor Wyngate's son, right?"

Now comes the calculation. My actual birth date is accessible to anyone with Google, but I'm pretty sure the steward doesn't care so long as I behave myself. Do I want the high-profile actress to know my secrets or do I want to engage in a few hours of flirting with an "older woman"? I could get huffy and tell her to go away, but where's the fun in that? I could pretend she's mistaken me and offer to buy her a drink. I could admit the truth and offer to buy her a drink. I could pretend I misunderstood the line of questioning and buy her a drink.

"Cosmopolitan, right?" I signal the steward, who indicates I can wait a moment. I smile with a slight nod.

"Not this early in the morning."

I could point out it must be night somewhere, but it technically is about four in the morning for those of us on London Time.

"Irish coffee then?"

"You *are* a bold one." I smile. She smiles back. Her pink lips invite kisses. I know nothing about her besides her movie, but I know she didn't grow up rich because her left bicuspid slightly pushes over the tooth in the front. I don't care about that. Kids who grew up in a more reality-based childhood tend to be more down-to-earth, is all. "Just coffee, no additives." She says this to the steward as he comes up beside her.

It wasn't like I was going to make it into the Mile-High Club if I plied her with enough adult beverages, so I wait for her to make the next verbal move.

"You noticed what I drink?"

She sure asks a lot of questions.

"Always been curious about what they taste like."

"Order one and find out."

"Can't. Allergic to limes."

"Seriously?" Her face sobers. "How did you find that out?"

"Drank a big glass of limeade after a mountain bike race. It wasn't the first time I'd drank limeade and I'd noticed it caused a tickle, but my throat closed down that time."

"Wow. So like what happens to people with bee stings?" I nod. "How old were you?"

"Middle school. Have not drank limes since."

"You haven't touched them in the last half-decade?" I smile at her because we both know she's trying to get me to admit my age.

"It's been longer." Barely. "My hands get itchy when I do." Not technically true. My hands get itchy from contact with lime juice. I have successfully cut limes for friend's margaritas by just touching the peel and then washing my hands immediately after. I'm not going to answer her query about my age and she seems to realize that.

"I guess your curiosity will have to remain unsatisfied."

"I guess." I smile slyly. "Unless the taste is worth the visit to the ER."

"It's not." She's got a tiny crease between her eyes. I've perhaps pushed it too far. Europe may have made me bolder than is wise.

"Then I guess I'll never know." I sigh, then shrug. I don't miss limeade, so I think I can live without satisfying my curiosity about cosmos. "Were you in Europe for a movie or fun?"

She chuckles.

"Most people think being an actress and fun are the same thing."

"It's your job. Are jobs fun?"

"I don't suppose you've ever had one."

Ouch! It's not my fault my dad has money.

"I'm in school."

"That's not the same thing." She's still smiling and I don't know where she's headed. No, I've never had a job. I expect I'll never need the money, but I kind of think I don't want to do nothing all my life either. My father, uncle, and grandfather have jobs after all. The steward sets a small tray with the coffee and sugar and cream on the table and asks if she needs anything else. She says no, sips her coffee and pins me with her bright blue eyes. "I saw your video."

Wow. Does everybody in the world have a Google alert for my name? If I rolled up to a village in the Amazon jungle, would they whip out a smartphone and show me a video of my finest hour?

"It's not my video. I didn't post it."

"No, but you feature in it. It's not like I film the movies I'm in. Did you enjoy your debut in film?"

I hated half the people in our hotel bringing it up.

"I would never put up a video like that."

"So, you're not a dick, just an ass." I blink at her. She keeps smiling as she breathes deeply in and out. Oh, baby, she does that well! "I'm not trying to be mean." She stares at me as I exercise my best poker face. I'm glad my book is on my lap. Can I feign annoyance while rising in her

6

presence? Wow, tough one! "And you are apparently mature enough to know that. Who was the guy with you?"

My cousin Collin interfered with my attempt to bribe the chick to delete the video. He pissed her off and guaranteed it was going on the Internet. Some versions of the video play the whole interaction.

"Collin's my cousin."

"Was he supposed to be your chaperone?"

"Not really, why?"

"He's just a dick …" She gives me a long side glance. "I hoped he wasn't a friend."

"You know what they say – you can choose your friends, but you're stuck with family." I'm not enjoying this conversation now, and I want to take a long pull off my drink, but she's watching me and that's not the time to be stupid. "And, you're right. He is a jerk, but my dad pushed him at me."

"Did he – Collin -- push all the ale on you?"

I smirk.

"Nah, I kind of did that to myself. British ale has a higher alcohol content than the beer I'm used to."

"Ah, which explains peeing in the fountain."

I can't help it. I blush. I was a little drunk that night, but mainly, I just really had to go to the bathroom.

"It wasn't my finest moment."

"Good you know that. So you asked me if my job is fun." She tilts her head like she contemplates her answer. She might have a future as an actress beyond action star. "It is and it isn't. When I first did 'Death Con', I thought I was having a great time. There was a lot of drinking and nobody said no to the 16-year-old. My off-camera behavior almost

7

cost me doing the second picture, so now I watch myself. I'll be legal to drink in the United States in January."

I'm not sure what to say to that. She was drinking underage just like me and she still drinks, though I think she stopped at one. She's headed somewhere and I haven't figured it out yet, so I let her continue.

"And I see a great-looking, otherwise intelligent guy making an ass of himself in a foreign country, clearly withdrawing from a binge on the plane, and then drinking bourbon for breakfast. I get it. Hair of the dog and all that. I just needed to say something."

She takes her coffee tray to her seat, leaving me with a very good reason *not* to have a third drink, which is kind of annoying. What's the use of flying Club class if you can't enjoy the adult beverages? I appreciate that British Airways recognizes me as an adult since my ID says I can vote and die in a war. I just wish everyone else would quit trying to make my decisions for me. I only drink the two straight-up bourbon-and-waters in the eight-hour flight across the Atlantic. I want a third and I'm nowhere near drunk, just mellowed enough *not* to get on another plane for Florida, to go visit my mother, who couldn't care less what I was up to in Europe. The dream reminds me she comes with her own complications. Facing the music that is my father is better for me. Just.

At the baggage carousel, I shoulder my backpack while looking for my duffle bag, hoping to avoid the paparazzi. Faint hope. They start snapping pictures and shouting at me the moment they see me. They can shout all the questions they want, but I'm not giving interviews, so they're wasting their breath. Yeah, yeah, my dad's the freaking governor. What does that have to do with me?

The vultures seem to think it has a lot to do with me. They're better than a chaperone most days because, since Dad became governor last fall, everything I do is now public. People can snap shots all day long, couple them with wild speculations and post it all on social media and bathroom walls without asking my dad's permission. I didn't realize until I ended up trending on Instagram a couple of weeks ago. Who knew anyone in London would even care who my dad is?

So, yeah, I disrupted polite English society for all of about ten minutes, but I did enough pub crawls to know there's a lot of blokes in the UK done the same thing and not ended up trending on Instagram. Dad's fame rubs off on me whether I like it or not and I really don't like it. Why can't the press and every guy or gal with a camera phone just leave me the hell alone?

I see my duffle bag emerge onto the conveyor but pull up short as a tall girl with buzzed dark hair and the most amazing blue-green eyes turns from the carousel as I step forward. She's wearing a black leather jacket that seems incongruous with the hiker's backpack she's swinging onto one slender shoulder. She's long and lanky with high cheekbones and full lips and her movements say she's a lot stronger than her frame suggests. Her eyes cast me a quick smile of sympathy before she disappears into the crowd, safe in her anonymity.

I hate cameras and reporters yelling at me. My stomach roils before I make it through the tight knot of paparazzi just outside the baggage pickup. Everybody wants to know about that stupid fountain. I drank too much, I couldn't find a bathroom and Collin encouraged me. It seemed like a good idea at the time. I wouldn't do it today. I don't say any of these things. I don't say anything at all. The family's driver, Vic, meets me just as I clear the worst of the crowd, steering me away from them. I glance around for that amazing girl, but she's already gone, almost as if I'd imagined her. Damn, she would have been on my flight, probably stuck back in steerage. Instead of flirting with Jorga and having bourbon for breakfast I could have enjoyed a conversation with her.

"How was your trip?" Vic keeps his voice low as we utilize our long strides to leave the shouting behind.

"Better now." Jorga appears atop the escalator and the paparazzi forget all about me. Vic's eyes twitter back toward the down escalator. Everybody wants to see the newest star of the latest film franchise, even the guy who's supposed to be driving me home from the airport. I don't care and wouldn't have noticed her except she sat right across the aisle from me in Club Class. She's pretty, but my god, she's nosey. But that girl with the eyes … the world is so unfair.

Vic knows his way around JFK and its parking garages and soon we're on the Long Island Expressway driving past familiar scenery.

"Is my dad home?" My stomach turns in anticipation of the answer.

"I think he's still in Albany."

Relief! I could easily forego the fatherliness. I relax into the leather of the Mercedes' back seat. I'm thirsty. I should have stopped at a water fountain on the way through the airport. The Mercedes SUV doesn't have a bar or mini-fridge, so I suck dust off my tongue for the entire 60 miles to the grey-shingled house on Shore Drive in Port Mallory. Think high-end Monopoly territory - North Carolina Avenue – swank without being ostentatious. The house sits on the right side of the road, literally and figuratively. The backyard allows access to the beach, which made me extremely popular in high school. Hell, I would have been popular anyway. I throw great parties and my dad's never home.

Besides being the current governor of New York, my father is also a businessman. We're rich, have been for generations. There was a big farm that -- cue snotty accent -- Great-Great-Grandfather sold off in parcels in the 1920s to grow several businesses that survived the Depression and then Great-Grandfather sold more in the 1950s to fund expansion of those businesses. We're the Long Island equivalent of the Cabots and Lodges of New England, except we're captains of industry, not political wannabes. My father is the first Wyngate to run for public office since some great-uncle was a road commissioner in the 1950s. I think Grandfather and Dad buy properties, but they also own manufacturing plants and some kind of transport company. The grand view lot we live on wasn't part of the original homestead. Europe gave me an eye for older architecture, so I look at the grey-shingled mansion as hopelessly new, a dime-a-dozen McMansion on steroids. Expensive materials don't create character. The "weathering" is painted on, not patina.

Vic pulls through the stone bollards at the end of the driveway and draws up to the portico before the front entrance. Yeah, I could order servants to grab my bags for me, but I never do. Carrying my duffle and backpack, I let myself into the house, my Vans squeaking on the flagstone floor in the double-height foyer with its attempt at old-world elegance – a black-iron chandelier and matching sconces, palm-wide door moldings, and stained-glass clearstories. I pause there a moment. It doesn't feel like home. I've been in hotels with more personal feeling. I can go straight to the living room, left into the den, or right, either down the corridor to the dining room and then into the kitchen or up the stairs. The house echoes with silence like nobody knows I've come home, so I climb the curving stairs to my room which overlooks the rose garden and the five-car garage. The house is too big for just four family and three servants (or is that three family and four servants? Collin would argue that Tilly is not a family member), but it provides us an abundance of individual privacy. If I threw a party when my dad was home and kept my guests away from his end of the house, he might not notice. That's how big this house is.

The thick wooden double-door to my bedroom is closed, but not locked, so I push in. Grey berbere carpet, a massive bed with a wooden headboard and matching footboard, matching linens in dark blue and palest grey greet me. This feels more like home because Dad let me choose the color pallet from some pre-approved choices the year I started high school. It's tasteful, but I would have preferred warmer colors. At least the furniture is warm woods.

I drop my bags on the blue-and-grey-striped loveseat and push open the matching drapes to let the sunshine in. My right eye dilates painfully, a reminder that I'm tired and started the day feeling punk. Still, I leave the draperies open while I unpack.

I unzip my bag to dump my dirty clothes in the hamper outside the bathroom, stowing the duffle neatly in the walk-in closet that is bigger than my friend Ben's entire bedroom. I'm pulling crap out of the backpack when Alyse comes in unannounced without knocking. Before I know it she launches herself into my arms, wrapping her legs around my hips. A combination of proximity alerts and hormones rage through my head.

"Hey, little sis. I have missed you."

Just turned fifteen, she's tall and willowy, a ballerina with long black hair, currently in a single wrist-thick braid over her left shoulder. She's been wearing it that way forever – at least since sixth grade. It's easy to coil up into a ballerina bun. I called her from Europe several times, but I might have gotten a little busy the last few weeks. Paris and London absorbed my attention. Guilt claws at me for leaving her hanging. Did I speak to her since I texted her just before boarding the ferry between Calais to Dover? Oops.

"I'm so glad you're back. Tilly's being a hag."

I set Alyse on the bed because holding her with her legs wrapped around my waist makes me … uh … anxious.

"Ally, come on. She's not that bad." I like Tilly. She's better than our bio mom. Maybe Alyse just doesn't remember what it was like when Laren lived here. Nine when Mom left, she's never visited her in Florida like I have. A couple of meals out every year or so isn't a fair comparison. Our family doesn't talk about it because it just stirs up bad memories. Maybe we should. If Alyse only knew what we're missing, she'd love Tilly too.

"She's not that bad to *you*. You're the golden boy."

Okay, Alyse loves me. And, Tilly has a lot of reason to like me. I'm a rich kid with class. I clean my room – mostly. I say 'please' and 'thank you'. I ask permission to do stuff – mostly. I get good grades considering I don't bother to study. I get straight A's when I do. Adults generally like me -- until they don't. Adults except for our dad who thinks I'm a blot on the family name. At least that's how he acts – always asking me what my plans are – as if I have any choice in *his* plan for my life.

Tilly's just trying to keep the peace so she can keep her job. That might be easier since he was elected governor. It's not like he can commute home from Albany if she quits. I'm an adult in all but birthdate and I'm not going to live in Dad's fishbowl, so keeping Tilly happy is high on my list too.

"What have you been up to?" I wriggle my neck out of Alyse's grasp so I can continue to unpack my bag. She really needs to stop draping herself over me. I started to feel weird about it last year, but now I'm downright uncomfortable. She became a woman over the last two months and, sister or not, I'm a guy. Yeah, I notice that her breasts are a little bigger and her dancer's butt is firm. I think about a pre-war Parisian *pissoir* I encountered to bring my anatomy under control. The visual and smell memory allows me to set down the backpack. "I've been schlepping around looking at old statues. Tell me you spent these weeks doing something more entertaining."

Okay, I didn't spend a lot of time looking at old statues. I maybe peed on a couple in that fountain. I liked the European buildings. Architecture could be my major. I'm an artist and good at math. Seems like a perfect fit to me. Dad will disagree that art is a job, but architecture .... I'm going to have to figure out a good argument to win him over.

"Ella's parents are getting divorced, so I spent most of it passing her Kleenex."

"Divorce sucks." It does. I've lived through it. Alyse might not remember and I don't want to stir up a hornet's nest. Ally's sly. She acts like I'm the best brother ever, but then she makes me pay for my part in the divorce. I told Alan about Laren and Sam having sex in his house. I guess you could view it as it's my fault they got a divorce, but really – our family values peace now in Laren's absence because she's gone. I can't remember a moment's peace before she left.

I sort through a stack of unopened mailer boxes with European stamps on my antique desk. Tilly understands that I want to give souvenirs to people myself. Last year I took a trip to Florida to see Mom. When I came home to find Tilly had given Ally her gifts – well, just say I can sulk like nobody's business. I open the box I sent from Vienna. Great, the Augarten porcelain looks perfect, nestled in its cotton wool and bubble wrap. I reclose the box and bring it to Alyse.

"For me?" Of course, for her. She's my only sister, so of course, for her. *Dancing Girl in Black and White* makes her gasp. It's just the kind of crap I know makes her day. I looked for a ballerina, but I know I made the right choice the minute I see her face. "It's so beautiful." Christmas dwells in her blue eyes. "You have such good taste." She kisses me on the cheek and warmth floods through my body. It's all shades of wrong, but holy shit! Her hand on my thigh makes me antsy, so I push off the bed to stow some more of my stuff. Concentrate on *anything* else.

"So, besides acting as Ella's cry rag, what did you do this summer?"

"Ben came over and we went swimming several times." Ben's my best friend, but he's been around for so long, Alyse thinks of him as a second brother. "You should call him. He's got a new girlfriend."

"Really? Someone from school?"

Last year Alyse and I attended the same school for the first time. Alyse notices things I don't and remains willing to share her observations. I learned a lot about my friends that I hadn't figured out on my own.

"Pamela Torneau."

Bottle-blonde hair, big hazel eyes. Pam's in our class. Was. We graduated in May. I'm the first Wyngate to graduate from a public school in three generations. Dad did public elementary school but then went to preparatory school for high school. Anyway, Pam plays tennis like Ben, so no surprise they'd hook up. I don't like it. I asked her out once a couple of years ago and she was rude. Girls can let you down gently or they can turn you down hard. Pam dropped me from 30,000 feet without throwing in a parachute. Still, she's fair game because I never dated her, which Ben knows. I wonder if he's getting any. Not my business, of course, but Ben deserves a good time.

Alyse continues to talk about her summer. She sounds lonely. She didn't make a lot of friends at school last year. She always attended Laurel Ridge Academy before middle school. When Ella, a friend all through elementary school, announced she was going to public high school, Alyse whined Dad into letting her go too. Whether in private school or public school, girls deeply envy Alyse while guys seem either intimidated or … well, Ben says she projects an unapproachableness. That's dancers. They exist in this world of performance where you can look, but not touch. That's a problem for high school guys who definitely want to touch. I prefer they don't touch my sister. My resistance may be part of the problem, but that's a dilemma she won't have this coming year.

A knock on my bedroom door interrupts us, so I call "come in." Tilly became our housekeeper before I can remember clearly before Laren left. She cooks, cleans and bandages my skateboarding scrapes. She also listens to me whine about Mom leaving, girls torturing me, and Dad never being home. I can't call her my stepmother because she's not married to my father and he left her with us when he went to Albany. I guess she's my non-bio mom. Maybe I should coin that phrase.

Short and trim, with capable hands, she wears her shining hair-colored hair in a no-nonsense bob. Although there's no uniform for household staff here, she always wears dark blue slacks (a skirt when the occasion allows) paired with a light blue shirt and comfortable brown shoes that are entirely unfashionable. She covers her ensemble with a dark blue cardigan on cool days or a dark blue suit jacket when out doing household business. I don't think she's ever been married, but she wears a ring on her left-hand wedding finger -- a simple silver metal with blue enameled etchings. She claims it's just jewelry, but I don't believe her. She doesn't even wear earrings while working, so why would she wear a just-jewelry ring? She can't be much over 30, if that, now that I think about it. Where does she go on her day off? Inquiring minds suddenly want to know.

"I missed you so much." I give her a hug which she semi-blocks by putting an arm across her chest before I draw her close to me. She started doing that when I hit high school, but I figured it out this summer. The attractive athlete – not her son – physical contact might stir up some emotions in a single female. The body and the head fight. Man, am I familiar with that! I release her but keep her in a sideways hug. She likes that better, her arm coming around my back. I'm tall, but she keeps her arm way above my butt.

"What have you been up to while I was gone?"

"The usual." She favors me with a bright smile. "Nothing as exciting as Europe."

I wonder if she's ever been. She's gone on two-week vacations occasionally, but she never seems to have gone anywhere interesting. Or does she just prefer not to tell us?

"Yes, Peter, tell us all about Europe." Alyse's twinkle encourages me to tell them about the whole fountain incident. I don't want to talk about that, so I launch into a story about the week in Monaco. Alan arranged for me to meet up with the son of one of his business acquaintances. The older brother he planned got delayed and so a college-aged sibling toured me around the principality. Francesca and I went to the topless beaches, toured the perfume streets and even gambled in one of the casinos.

That reminds me of the gift I got Tilly and I go find the box from Monaco. It's a de Grasse that smells like jasmine. She thanks me profusely as Alyse glares on. Tilly senses the tension, slides the bottle into her pocket and tells me to go on with my story.

Francesca plied me with plenty of Chateau Margaux Bordeaux but still didn't get me into her bed. At least I think I'd remember if we'd done the deed. Wouldn't the body remember?

"Peter, I don't like where this story is going." Tilly frowns when I reach the whole drinking-at-the-Wine-Palace-and-coming-home-to-a-darkened-palazzo part of the story. "You need to be thinking about your future and that can lead to places you don't want to go."

True, but I fear dying the only male virgin over the age of 16 on Long Island. She's right, of course, and I've avoided hookups for that reason. Morality isn't getting me laid any quicker, however, so I'm rethinking that strategy. I just need the right girl. Someone who wants to fool around without planning a wedding, someone I can trust to be on the pill and not allergic to condoms.

"I have to get back to work." She looks at her phone. "The grocer is in the driveway. Will you be awake for dinner or do you expect jetlag to hit you hard?"

"I'm good. Just going to take a shower and relax, maybe take a short nap."

"Maybe brush your teeth." Tilly winks at me before going out the door.

Damn. I guess the bourbon worked its way through the toothpaste I used on the plane. Alyse stands up and retrieves her figurine from the nightstand.

"I'm going now. I think you've probably been up a while."

"About twenty hours. I'm so happy to be back."

She hugs me and leaves me alone. The clock makes a loud ticking noise. I open more souvenir boxes and line them up on the desk to give them to people. Time's passing. Clock's ticking. I feel itchy. All organized, I take a shower, staring at this thin face with high cheekbones and enormous green eyes that fill the shaving mirror I decide not to use. I don't really like scruff, but I'm too tired to risk a razor near my jugular. The green of my eyes startles against my black hair. Wrapped in a robe, I text Ben.

PETER Pamela Torneau, huh? Tell me all about it.

Ben's my best friend. I started kindergarten in public elementary school a year before I was supposed to because I passed some tests that said I was ready. When I got there, my classmates knew I was different and kids don't treat difference kindly. It wasn't that I was physically smaller than my classmates or that my brain was bigger than theirs. I was physically coordinated for all that I was shorter and I quickly figured out not to be a know-it-all in class. That wasn't what kept them at bay. I came from a different world – practically another planet. Yeah, there were plenty of rich kids in Port Mallory, but they all went to Xavier Academy or Laurel Ridge Academy. Alan insisted on public school and Laren relented. I didn't know why wealth made me an outcast, and my mom wasn't sympathetic to my tears. It could have been a miserable year, except for Ben.

Ben liked me – or he's really the nicest guy in the world. When I showed him I could hang upside down from the monkey bars just as long as he could and not turn green, he declared me his best friend. His friendship changed my school experience. We played together the next summer at the property my dad owns across the street from Ben's house. After that, people didn't treat me like Richie Rich anymore – at least not until high school when they realized the advantages my father's wealth could purchase. That's a whole different set of prejudices that I don't object to.

Except for a few trips, my exile to boarding school in sophomore year and these last couple of months in Europe, I've hung out at Ben's house almost every day as far back as I can remember. It's how I learned about normal life. His family raised me -- took me to movies, swimming at the lake – his mom taught me to ride a bike – his father discussed sex with me. The desire to see Ben and his family outweighs my exhaustion.

I walk out to the garage and pull the tarp off my Porsche. Its rich purple gleams in the sunlight, making my scratchy eyes burn and water. I love driving that car, feeling the power through the palms of my hands, lower back, and feet, hearing its throaty purr. I'm not feeling the thrill today. My skin crawls and my throat feels coated in vomit. The low-level headache still throbs behind my right eye. I feel like crap and only my homesickness to see Ben gets me behind the wheel of the car.

I drive with the windows down and my head clears along the way. The sun lights the trees too brightly and traffic moves too fast. Fortunately, from our house to Ben's is all surface roads. Even so, some guy pulls out from a stop sign without enough room and I momentarily envision punching his face in.

Home

Ben

I'm working on my blue Jeep in the driveway when Pete pulls up on the street, against the Rose of Sharon hedges on the far side of the road. I'm surprised to see him, even though he said he was coming. When you know Pete for a while, you learn not to trust him about keeping his promises or following schedules. It's just not in his personality to be that organized. He makes up for it by being scrupulous with money, unlike most of the rich kids I know. He doesn't shove his wealth in your face, but he pauses and considers whether I can afford something he wants to do before he suggests it. He used to offer to treat until I got prickly about it once and now he's even less pushy about it than he was before. He never welshes on a bet and if he walks out without his wallet and I have to pay, he reimburses and rounds up.

He sweeps his arms wide while crossing the street, clearly glad to be home. Those Sharon blossoms scent the air with sweet perfume. Against the blue sky, Pete looks utterly alive – charged with electricity, almost too bright – but in the moment.

"You didn't go to bed." Pete's an inch taller than me, black hair and emerald eyes to my light-brown hair and hazel eyes. He's handsome and girls react to him like catnip, but I'm better with people than he is – girls like me as a friend and guys are envious of him. He cares about that, not seeking to alienate people. There are all kinds of reasons to like Pete.

"I need to." His blood-shot eyes look fevered. "I wanted to see you before I crash. Unfortunately, I left your gift at the house."

"Welcome home." I wipe the grease off my fingers so we can embrace. I couldn't care less about the gift. He'll remember to bring it next time. "How was your trip?"

He apologized via text once during his trip. Internet in Europe is hit and miss, so he claimed. Pete's self-centered and when he recognizes that, he's sorry for it, but he doesn't ever seem to learn from it long-term. He'll revert to self-centered whenever he's distracted by shiny objects.

"Lots of old buildings and dope babes."

"Trust you to find those."

His cheeks flush. Everybody thinks Pete's a ladies' man, but he doesn't end up with any of the ones that hang around him. Standing next to him is a good way to get the girls he doesn't want and some of them are beautiful. Yeah, Pete can get a date whenever he wants – it's that second date that doesn't ever seem to happen. Although there are girls who claim they've had sex with him, Pete denied it last year. I wonder if he crossed the great divide in Europe, but I feel awkward asking. It's not cool in our class for guys to have standards rather than a string of hookups and I don't want to be alone in the Brotherhood of Celibacy.

He tells me about Trajan's Market and the Baths of Diocletian. He seems to have enjoyed southern Europe. I ask him about the Eiffel Tower, which excites my engineering soul. His eyes turn leftward.

"Parisian girls think they're all that. So, what were you doing this summer?"

He just tried to distract me. What the hell did he do in Paris if he wasn't seeing the sights? If he didn't see the Eiffel Tower, he couldn't have seen much.

"I'm working over at Temple Manufacturing, on their loading dock, and then on the weekends with Captain Russell."

Pete's mouth tightens. Not that he wants to get all sweaty and dirty lifting that barge and toting that bale, but he regrets that I have to work. A couple of times when he's been drunk, he's said he feels essentially useless and predicts, when I figure it out, I'll leave like his mom did and he'll be alone again. His lack of any real purpose in life worries me for him, but it doesn't matter to our friendship. He's almost a year younger than me and he doesn't have to do anything because of all his dad's money. He'll get tired of that eventually and make it up – once he realizes it's completely in his control to do.

"Ally told me you've been dating Pamela for a month now."

"Yeah. She's been fun."

He's skeptical and I know why. Pam likes movies and hanging out at the coffee house. I prefer more active entertainments – mountain biking and sailing. No girlfriend has ever wanted to join me on those adventures, so yeah, my relationships never last long, though always longer than his. Pamela and I play tennis a lot and I just tolerate the coffee house.

"She's headed to Brown in a few weeks."

"Well, that sucks."

"Nah. Plenty of fish in the sea and I'm sure there'll be plenty at Dartmouth." I earned a partial scholarship to Dartmouth, but the loans I'll have to take out to close the gap terrify. I don't expect I'll have much time for socializing between school and work. "Any chance we can go mountain-biking later this week? I've got some days free while they retool the production line."

"Yeah, absolutely. It's going to be weird being at Yale and you're up in New Hampshire."

"It will. There's got to be a midpoint we can meet at."

"I'll just drive up every few weeks. It's what – three hours? That's got to be an adventure. And the White Mountain ski lodges will be well worth it."

"You sure? I mean, I hardly heard from you this summer."

I stung him. I'm supposed to believe he got busy and connectivity was an issue. Or pretend. He'd settle for pretend.

"My dad sent Collin to chaperone me, so I just didn't have a lot of free time."

He apologizes, explaining his good intentions were subject to his cousin's party nature, causing him to roll out of bed groggy and hungover, spend a few hours rushing around whatever city to fulfill his dad's requirements, sometimes get on a train that moved too fast to enjoy the scenery and then spend the evening clubbing, only to roll into bed exhausted and get up a few hours later to do it all over again. Sounds like he repeated boarding school except in French.

By the time he's finished telling me about all his adventures, he's leaning on my car, about ready to fall asleep on his feet. He insists he's not bipolar, but his mother is and sometimes I wonder. He's really good at ignoring exhaustion, but he's clearly hitting a wall. His voice sounds like gravel.

"So you pretty much spent the last two months drunk or hungover. I guess that explains London."

"Heard about that, huh?"

"It made Instagram and Twitter, then it made it to Facebook and the gossip sites. And, everybody who saw it for the first time texted me because your phone wasn't working."

He groans in embarrassment. Pete insists it didn't start out to be a spectacle. They were in a pub, one among many, and he couldn't get into the loo. That's what they call the restroom there.

"It's easier to say than 'bathroom' and I've noticed the English like easy words, unlike the rest of Europe. The ale raped my kidneys, so I couldn't wait for the next pub. I turned into an alley to avoid wetting my pants and we found the fountain at the other end."

The ale might have overwhelmed his good sense. At least he can admit it.

"It seemed like a good idea until this chick started filming us. I tried to charm her. I even offered her money to delete it, but she knew who I was and there was nothing I could do to stop her from posting it on the Internet."

"You were lucky you didn't get arrested. London has laws, you know?"

"Nobody called the cops. What's the fun in that? Cops ruin the party."

Okay, he's scaring me. He usually knows there are laws for a reason if his friends sometimes have to explain the reason to him. He shrugs.

"Dad wasn't happy. He didn't make me come back, but he threatened. If I hadn't of been with Colin, I think he'd have been more upset."

I refrain from comment, asking him if he wants some lemonade. There was a time when I believed Pete was influenced by his cousin or Trevor Grey to drink too much. I now know he likes getting drunk and doesn't need their influence anymore if he ever did. We head into the house. It's too early to see my dad, but my mom chops carrots at the counter. A teacher, she doesn't start work for a couple more weeks. I stare at a pitcher of limeade in the fridge, before pulling lemonade out of the freezer.

"I can have water, Ben. It's fine." Pete does try to be a low-maintenance friend and his allergy isn't his fault. My stomach still clenches when I remember the terror we all felt when he couldn't breathe. His lips were blue by the time the ambulance got there and I thought I'd caused that. It was nobody's fault and I'm maybe too accommodating of his allergy because of that long-ago event.

"It's all plastic." He doesn't know what that means, and his face doesn't relax when I put the container in the microwave. Okay, maybe he thinks I'll serve it warm. There's some normal-life things he just doesn't get. Servants probably do this at his house all the time, but he isn't there for it, so he doesn't know. Next time, it'll make sense to him.

"Hey, Helen." Pete gives my mom a sideways hug. She sets down her knife and embraces him with both arms. Mom's tried to fill the void in Pete's life left by his mother's departure and even before. He seems to need it and I don't resent it. This summer was the first time since his involuntary semester at boarding school that he's not been at our house at least five days a week. Mom's eyes twitter over his shoulder before she pulls back from the hug and stares into his eyes.

"Have you been drinking?"

No way! He can't be that stupid!

"Um, in Europe, sure. Laws are different there." He's that stupid.

"No, I mean today. I can smell it on your breath."

"That's mouthwash."

He's lying. I know he's lying and Mom -- she has a superpower – bullshit detector. I know better than to even try and she's sniffed out Pete's attempts like a bloodhound. He ought to know better.

"Way too young," she chides, tucking a brown lock behind her ear since it came loose of her ponytail. "Did you drive over?"

"I'm not drunk, Helen." Pete's tired and it makes him irritable. He keeps his tone light, but the message is clear.

Back off! "You want to Breathalyze me?" Really? He's usually smoother than that. She's frowning and her eyes gleam. He's stung her.

"I want you to be smart, Peter." Her voice grows hoarse. "Drunk driving isn't smart."

"I'm not drunk. Seriously? Americans are so uptight about drinking. In England, everybody drinks and nobody acts like it's a big deal for guys my age to have a few in an evening." He's not winning her over and Pete is good at reading adults. It's our age group he struggles with. "But I'm not legal to drink this side of the Atlantic, so you won't have to worry about it."

Somehow word never gets back to our parents that Pete's parties are blowouts because of the beer and wine. He doesn't cater it, but plenty of people bring cannabis and booze too. Nobody wants to ruin a good thing. Pete insists his dad ignores it because their house has no near neighbors to complain about the noise and Pete gets straight As. At least my parents care. Pete looks her directly in the eye and plays his trump card.

"I promise you that I am not driving drunk."

Mom sighs and turns back to her dinner prep. She doesn't believe him, but it's not like she can just call up his father and out him. She used to have that power over him, but since his dad's in Albany now, he knows she can't. All she can do is try to guide Pete and she can't do that if she alienates him. I know what she's thinking because she'll say exactly that to me after he leaves. It won't be the first time. I hand him an iced glass of lemonade.

"Are you staying for dinner?" Mom asks.

He takes a moment to answer, covering his irritation with a gulp of lemonade.

"Nah. I should probably go home and catch some zzz's."

Clattering sounds at the backdoor and Wes comes barreling in, 10 years old, covered in scabs, hair practically to his shoulders. He was the surprise child. After my sister died of an undiagnosed heart problem just before I started kindergarten, my parents fooled around and had Wes. I love him, but eight years is a huge gap.

"Hey, shaggy." Pete and I tried to grow our hair that long one year, but his is naturally curly and conspired into a nest he couldn't get a comb through. It only got worse as the summer grew more humid. He's kept it short ever since and it's a good thing he's rich because he spends a fortune in product in the summer to keep it from frizzing.

"Pete! You're back!" They hug. Pete's been around Wes's whole life, as much a brother as me. He's even taken him fishing when I've been out of town. That's why I returned the favor with Alyse this summer, even though I don't like hanging out with her. This summer she really creeped me out a few times with some clumsily-executed sexual innuendos.

"Just flew in a couple of hours ago. What you been up to?"

"Nothing. There's nobody my age around here." Wes complained most of the summer about being bored. When Pete and I were his age, there were a million kids our age living in the houses around here. I think there probably still are, but sometimes you have trouble connecting with people you could call friends. "I was checking out the house next door. The Carsons moved out, so it's for sale."

"That was that old couple, right?" A lot of guys our age would ignore the little brother, but Pete genuinely cares what the kid's been up to. It's a paradox how he can sometimes be so cavalier with friends his own age and yet intensely interested in the activities of a 10-year-old. Not to mention that he knows who lived next door. How does that work?

"Right."

"They're moving to Florida," Mom explains. "Since their kids moved to other states to get away from the taxes, it just seemed like it was time to go. The house went on the market today."

I've seen that look on Pete's face before whenever either of our fathers starts talking about taxes. I doubt it matters to Alan Wyngate personally. He has plenty of money to live on. He's philosophically opposed to taxes for other reasons I don't understand. My dad brings it up to Pete because maybe he hopes he'll influence the governor. Pete doesn't understand and is the first to admit he has no influence over his father, especially on a topic like taxes, which he knows nothing about. His ignorance seems willful. Pete is smarter than that, but when he doesn't want to learn something, there's no changing his mind.

"Who wouldn't want to live through another Long Island winter?" Pete's joke turns into a jaw-cracking yawn. "I really should get going." He gulps the last of the lemonade, yawns again and moves toward the door. I follow. Pete walks faster than anyone that tired should. Could be the sugar. "I missed your birthday and the 4th of

July, but maybe we can get everybody together before we head for school."

"Sounds good." I turned 18 a few weeks ago, but Pete's nearly 10 months younger because his mother pushed for him to start school early. He yawns again as we walk toward his car. Maybe I should try to talk him out of driving. I hesitate as he gets into the Porsche, the lowering afternoon sun filtering through the hedge behind him. He winces as if from a headache.

"You okay?" I ask. He laughs.

"Just tired. I'll call you when I wake from the coma."

He starts his car. He shouldn't be driving. I want to say that, but I don't. There's a lot I should say that I haven't. He pulls away and I watch him go, a check on my spirit that I choose not to respond to.

Sunrise Commune

Peter

Pouring coffee with one hand and rubbing my eyes with the other, I stare into the dewy morning. I'm never up at this hour, but it's the middle of the night in London, so my body's completely out of kilter. After 10 hours of coma, I woke to the predawn and couldn't go back to sleep. Fortunately, Tilly strives to be a good role model, so she got up early to make coffee. I haven't even showered yet, but after wearing the same three pairs of space-age undies for two months with just an occasional wash-and-drip, I'm a lot less fastidious than before.

The distant murmur of the ocean keeps me company as I settle into a lawn chair to watch the sun come up. The motion detector lights come on as soon as I step out of the kitchen door, but they cycle off after I sit down in the lawn glider. My eyes adjust to the dimness in time to note the lightening in the eastern sky. I love sunrises and sunsets, though I see sunsets more often. I lean back in the glider, the coffee balanced on my thigh to watch the sky grow pearly grey before a thin line of lighter blue appears on the horizon. Rosy pinks and sandy yellows welcome a new day. I imagine the sky as a sleepy eye opening as night bows off the stage as the day awakens. The canopy of scattered clouds blushes a mango orange, sending shimmering threads over the placid ocean. God waves His wand and the clouds glow tangerine, warming my soul and tickling my artist's mind. Last summer, I got up several times to catch this glory. A cool wind tugs at my sweatshirt and teases my hair in musical silence, and the sky opens up blue, like a fresh page awaiting ink. The leaves shed their grey for green and the outline of the lawn objects becomes clearer.

I enjoyed waking up in my familiar bed this morning. Travel disturbs my sleep as much as boarding school did. My headache is gone and for the first time in weeks, I don't have a pain in my upper gut. I'm still nauseous – a little – but that's probably a travel hangover. Breakfast appeals for the first time in months. When I finish my cup of coffee and sunrise commune, I'm going to ask for it. I'm absorbed by watching the silvery ocean mist burn off in the warm light of day.

A noise alerts me to Tilly setting the patio table. I get up to tell her she doesn't need to do that on my account. She should know that I'm low maintenance, but she's had two months with drama queen Alyse.

"Your father arrived last night," she announces with a smile. "You should go get cleaned up. He'll want to see you."

Thereby ruining any thought of breakfast.

I drain my cup. My stomach clenches into a fist. I take the backstairs up to my room to avoid dear ole Dad. I hang out in the shower longer than necessary. My hands shake while I shave. My neck muscles tighten and my head begins to throb. On my way to brushing my teeth, I dig through the shelves in the dressing room until I find a bottle of bourbon I hid there before I left for Europe. I take a long two-swallow slug, embracing the burn. I want more as warmth spreads through my chest and relaxes my shoulders, but I know better than to step over the edge from relaxed to wasted. I brush my teeth with a lot of paste and swish with mouthwash before donning nice jeans and an Oxford shirt to head downstairs.

Alan doesn't look up from his laptop when I slide into the seat across from him. He certainly doesn't notice my hands shake as I pour myself orange juice and another cup of coffee.

"Any idea where your sister is?" Alan's gaze never leaves his laptop as Tilly serves our plates.

"I knocked on her door, sir. I think I woke her." Alan genuinely smiles at her.

"Thank you, Tilly, for trying to roust that lay-a-bed, but I was asking Peter."

Why? Is it my day to watch Alyse and nobody informed me?

"I went to bed pretty early last night. I didn't talk to her after I got back from Ben's."

The omelet looks perfect, but my stomach incinerates the toast I nibble, so the peppers I love are going to make me sick.

"Just so you know, your little indiscretion in London might have prevented your matriculation at Yale."

Yeah, there's a good reason to drink hard liquor before breakfast. We talked over the phone when the story first broke. I admitted I was an idiot. He agreed with me. Bringing it up again annoys me.

"Oh, dear, then maybe I could go to a college I want to go to."

Alan looks over the laptop screen now. His brown hair lies perfectly in place and his blue eyes are sharp and clear. He wears a blue button-down, the collar open. It's the most relaxed I've seen him in months. Well, more than months. A year? He closes the laptop, puts it in the fourth chair with his leather briefcase. What ... I actually matter? Not likely.

"You've got a lot of potential, son. Don't waste it."

Bourbon gives me courage.

"Wouldn't it be wasting my potential if I major in things I'm not interested in?"

"We've discussed this." No, he's lectured me and I've listened. That's not a discussion. "You want to be a renaissance man, you do that on your own time. I'll pay for it so long as you're pursuing a useful degree as your main course. In the meantime, I don't want any more shenanigans. You need to learn to think ahead before you do things. I've tried to keep you and Alyse out of the public eye, but I can't prevent the paparazzi from paying attention when you do crazy things."

"I know." I know I wouldn't matter to the press if he wasn't the governor. Would I matter to him if he wasn't governor? Did I matter before? I wish I remembered.

"Do you? When you turn 18 in March, I won't be able to quash videos of you being stupid. You are smarter than that video."

That he tried to quash the video is news to me. Whatever he tried didn't work since everybody seems to have seen it.

"I'm 17. How smart am I supposed to be?"

He sighs.

"You are the son of the governor of New York. What do you think?"

I sigh now. The conversation ends because Alyse floats out of the living room and takes the empty seat with the unused table setting. Tilly whisks out a fresh pot of coffee and a bowl of yogurt and fruit.

"Is that all you're eating?" Alan asks.

"I've got dance camp this morning. Can't dance on a full stomach."

"How are you getting there?" Like he cares.

"I'll drive her." Alan raises an eyebrow at me. "Don't you need to get back to Albany?" Please, go back to Albany.

"I do, but I was hoping to spend a few hours with my children – especially you since you've been away." Oh, lucky me! "You haven't even told me about your trip."

When was I supposed to do that?

"What's to tell? The most interesting part played on TMZ."

"Surely, you did something more interesting than peeing in a fountain."

Alyse almost sprays me with yogurt. I won't talk about the more interesting parts of my trip. Dad won't approve of Monaco and my stomach is touchy enough without poking the stuffed shirt. I go with the potential for laughter.

"Amsterdam was entertaining."

Alan blinks at me, then shoots a look sideways at Alyse.

"Daddy, I know what happens in Amsterdam. I'm a dancer." She's right. I knew what to expect because of the pseudo-sophistication of dancers. Let's get this straight. High-school dancers *think* they are sophisticated as they troll the Internet to learn about all the places they aren't allowed to go to on their own. I knew what to expect, but I wasn't prepared for what I found.

"How did you manage to get a taxi driver to take a juvenile to De Wallens?"

He's been?! I didn't see that coming.

"Dad, come on. You know I hooked up with people who are older than me. Collin was with me, right?" Yeah, he might as well know that Collin wasn't the best role-model. I kept myself out of trouble better without him. No peeing in fountains in Monaco or Italy, for example. Yeah, I had a lot of wine that one night with Francesca, but I ate three meals a day and never ended up puking my guts out at the end of an evening. "Besides, when you're almost 6'1" people tend to think you're older than you are, especially if you don't shave for a week or so." I shaved. Nobody seemed concerned about me checking out the red light district. I suspect I could have sampled the wares without anyone raising an eyebrow. The thought of sharing a girl with the highest bidder kind of creeps me out.

"What did you think?"

"Degrading – treating women like objects." I want to be sophisticated about it, but it deeply bothers me that women's sexual favors are for sale on a street corner. It bothered me even as my erection was ripping my jeans. That's the Andersons' influence on me. He's nodding like he appreciates I have morals. He might as well know the whole of it. "And men kept pulling up to the curb and asking me if I was for sale, which – yeah." I shudder. Time to change the subject. "Collin liked the pot cafes."

"Oh, god! I thought you'd learned your lesson after that suspension."

"I did, and I didn't imbibe. I don't like pot that much." Alyse studiously avoids eye contact. I'm not going to tell Dad the pot was hers. I've already served my sentence in exile for that and I will go to my grave protecting her secret. It's good to see Alan willing to laugh about it now. When I screw up, I've got the worst timing. He'd just been asked to run for governor. That lawyer did a good job keeping it covered up.

"I've got to get going," Alyse announces.

I've eaten about two bites of my breakfast, but Mrs. Sims will have my left nut if Alyse is late, so I wipe my mouth with my napkin.

"I'll meet you at the car."

Alyse floats away into the house and I stand, but Alan's staring at me. his gaze holding me in my place while Alyse is free to flit as she will.

"What?"

"Did you have a good time?"

"Yeah, some of it was really cool. I loved the architecture and some of the cultural customs were fascinating." We saw Morris Dancers in a village north of London and gypsies somewhere on the mainland. "I wanted to climb the mountains in Switzerland. Unfortunately, I didn't have time."

"Maybe next summer. Good grades deserve rewards."

"Yeah?" But I'm not to be rewarded by going to a college of my own choosing. Got it. "I better get going."

"Oh, and you should swing by your grandparents' in the next few days. Dad's been asking about you."

Grunting that I will, I climb the back stairs three at a time to brush my teeth again and swish some mouthwash just in case people are smarter than Alan.

Alyse sits in the passenger seat when I get to the garage. She's worried about being late, so I take the shortest route and don't let the speed limit signs intimidate me.

Dance Theater Port Mallory

Peter

I get Alyse to Dance Theater Port Mallory in time to make it to her class, but she still manages to be five minutes late on the floor, tying her toe-shoes as Mrs. Sims and the rest of the class wait for her. Apparently, she's more talented than I was, because she can get away with that crap. Meanwhile, the girl on the desk scowls at her with that judgy look that I waver on. Be on time, little sis. Don't make me break the speed limit so you can play prima donna when you get here. On the other hand, don't glare at my sister like you're a robin and she's the worm. Well, unless you're hot, which this dancer surely is. I gather Alyse's abandoned dance bag and set it in a locker along the front wall.

"You're back." I frown at the lobby jockey before recognition dawns in my admittedly jet-lagged brain.

"Sue, right?"

"Cheyenne. Chy. I thought you were headed to Europe."

"Just back yesterday. And, I'm sorry. We know each other from school, right?"

"Well, more from here. We did hip-hop together."

I frown again, but the image that springs to mind makes me smile.

"You had purple hair then."

"Yes! With a streak of pink, I think."

Her hair is now a mass of hi- and low-lights falling to her shoulders, still curled by the ballerina bun it was released from. I stopped dancing when I went to boarding school. I still watch Alyse at practice sometimes, but I don't want to rejoin the studio. Some people think maybe it's because I'm out of shape, but I'm not. Alyse makes me practice with her sometimes. I just don't want to be tied down by the all-consuming discipline of dance.

"How was it?"

"It?"

"Europe."

"European. A lot of big old cities connected by fast-moving trains running past vineyards you couldn't see because you were going so fast."

"You get to see the Alps?"

"That was cool. Those are some amazing mountains. Make the Adirondacks look like hills."

"So, what was your favorite city?"

Nobody's asked me that before. Favorite city?

"I don't know. I liked the architecture, but not all of it in every city and – yeah."

"You traipsed around Europe and you didn't do anything fun?"

"Oh, sure. I did a lot of fun things – mostly at night. Europe has some cool nightlife and they aren't so fussy about the drinking age."

"I have been to a couple of your parties." She leans in toward me. I examine her face carefully before pulling back, careful to continue smiling. She's pretty, with a small blemish-free face and kissable pink lips. I just don't like to be close enough that I'm swapping CO_2 with someone I've just met.

"Yeah. I'm having another one."

"When?" Her hazel eyes briefly hide behind her mascaraed lashes.

I pull my phone out of my pocket, tap in my security code then look at her. She tells me her phone number and a moment later, she gets a message.

PETER - This is Peter. Get ready for a good time. Coming soon.

I'm hungry and still weirdly tired. I turn to leave. "Where you going?"

"I need some coffee. You want to come with?"

"I'm on the front desk."

While I'd rather she came with me, Ben has taught me that ordinary people (aka, those whose fathers aren't the governor of New York) need their jobs, so I ask her what she wants. While I wait in the drive-thru at Starbucks, I look in the glove box and the console. A water bottle awaits, reminding me of how I got through everybody staring at me at graduation. After a moment's hesitation, I ignore it. I should probably take it in the house when I get home, just in case I'm ever pulled over.

I return to DTPJ twenty minutes later carrying two venti cups, handing her the Americano. Dancers don't do fat, but they love their caffeine. We watch through the large glass window as Alyse and her fellow dancers choreograph a complicated performance they'll present next Friday evening.

"Why'd you quit dancing?" Cheyenne asks. Yeah, good question.

"It got boring." She raises an eyebrow. "I'm not saying *you* are boring. *I* got bored doing it. But we did a lot of dancing in Europe. That was fun. No schedules or doing the same move over and over."

"But you can do that because you did the same move over and over again."

She's got a point. I became partner bait in every disco we went to in Europe because I *know* how to dance. Collin took a couple of those girls to his hotel room. I kissed several, but it just moved too fast for me.

"Maybe, but it just quit being fun. If it's still fun for you, keep doing it. You and Alyse are beautiful."

"Why, thank you, sir." She curtsies, then looks out from under her mascara, her hazel eyes shining. She winks. "We'd be more beautiful with guys who could lift us."

I laugh, feeling my cheeks grow warm. If I'd known about the dating benefits at the time, I would maybe have opted for boredom.

Alyse's class ends and she comes running over in her toe shoes to give me a hug, which I straight-arm because – well, it's hard to get a date when people think you're coupled with your sister, something I'm only now realizing. My cheeks burn. While Alyse dons street clothes over her leotard, I talk with Cheyenne a bit more, lingering even after Alyse is ready to go. Cheyenne's funny. I'm surprised I didn't know that before. Alyse comes storming over.

"Peter, we have to go." She grabs my arm and drags me away.

"Bye, Cheyenne." I call the farewell over my shoulder as Alyse drags me through the door. I really have to make her stop this. Yeah, lunch, but for heaven's sake. Why all the fuss?

"Where to?" I ask because she has bounced over to my car.

"Someplace with meat and veggies."

Alyse has the toned body of a dancer, but like many of the girls, she avoids carbs like the plague. I suggest the Tiger Lily Café, which is so close that walking is faster than driving.

"So what's with the rudeness back there?" I ask as we walk. East Main is an older road with buildings right on the narrow sidewalk which is shaded with trees. I like the wood-frame buildings I've never noticed before. The sidewalk is set pavers rather than poured concrete. Some of the businesses have their own red-brick walks spreading out to meet the city's light-grey pavers.

"I'm hungry and I have to be back there at one o'clock."

"I thought you and Cheyenne were friends."

"Dancers aren't really friends, silly." Her delicate forehead wrinkles. "We're competitors. She got the role in *Babes in Toyland* I wanted."

Cheyenne is three years older and just as talented. Of course, she got the lead role. Alyse always pushes beyond her place. She'll get to dance the role the next time around ... unless she blows it with prima donna behavior.

"Sucks to be you, I guess." She frowns at me. I refuse to feel guilty. I am guilty, but – yeah. Not my fault.

We both know the Tiger Lily Café's menu so order food before even taking a table in the attached atrium. The Tiger Lily used to be an automotive shop, but it's been thoroughly remodeled, leaving the fine old details of a 1920s building combined with modern elements like the extruded aluminum atrium. I explain we're on a deadline and pre-tip, so we're served quickly. Alyse curls her lips in disgust at my sandwich.

"You're going to get fat eating all those carbs."

"I got so sick of listening to dancers harp on me. I've gained two and a half inches since I stopped dancing and only twenty pounds. I bet I lost five on this trip."

"Oh, come on, all that rich European food."

"I mostly drank my calories, thank you very much."

I mean it as a joke. We did a lot of walking in Europe and the rich food upset my stomach, so I ended up eating a lot of protein bars. But, yeah, the Europeans offer wine with just about every meal except breakfast and half the hotels offer mimosas or the much-preferable bellinis then. We drank a lot of alcohol – a lot more than I was used to. I hadn't drank every day since boarding school.

Alyse cocks her head sideways, her fork poised over her salad – lemon juice dressing, olives, eggs, mushrooms and pears over greens.

"You okay?" Her expression reads perplexed concern.

"Yeah, why wouldn't I be?"

"I don't know. I've been thinking about Uncle Matthew."

Our mother's brother died this spring from liver failure. He'd only been 35.

"I don't have Hep C, little sister."

"Is that what Mom said he had? Coz the magazine article I read said it was drinking – two trips to rehab 10 and 15 years ago."

"Nobody's liver gets that polluted from alcohol at 35. Besides, do I look sick?"

"No. Just … be careful, okay."

"I will. I am. Better finish your salad so you can get back to the studio."

"And what are you doing today?"

I suspect admitting I hope to hang out with Cheyenne will make the rest of lunch uncomfortable, so I come up with a different plan which can always be rewritten if I get a better offer.

"Thought I'd take the speed boat out, just make sure everything's running good for the weekend."

"You'd better take me out on it."

I grin at her. I like making her happy. I'd prefer to take a bunch of the guys, but of course, Alyse needs to be part of it because … well, she just does. That's been how it is since Ben and I ditched her about five years ago. She got lost in the woods and when she finally came out at the bridge her face was tear-streaked, smeared with snot and dark with rage. I didn't care then, but the next day, I felt lower than a Dachshund when she developed the red rash of poison ivy on both legs and one arm. Dad and Tilly *both* yelled at me that time. I've felt guilty about that ever since and try to include Alyse as often as I can. Still, now I sit back in my seat and half-assed pray that I meet Cheyenne in the lobby, and she'll have the afternoon free.

Now Starring Peter Wyngate

Cheyenne

Peter Wyngate is delicious – tall, athletic, still has the margins of a dancer's body. I bet he could get back in shape with only a semester of training. His green eyes shock you because his hair and lashes are so dark and they're enormous compared to his face. He smiles easily and his humor is quick and intelligent.

We attended school together, of course, but we *know* each other from dance. I don't think he remembers that we were paired as the Angel and the Troll King. He never got to dance the role. I don't know why. He went somewhere for a while and then came back, but he never came back to the studio except to watch his sister dance.

My little brother Josh is waiting for me with his trombone case in hand. He climbs into the back seat, which tells me he doesn't want to talk. I think we last had a conversation in March. He asked if I knew where our older brother Chas was. I don't recall if I did or not. When you're 15, you don't talk to your sister very often. It's a thing. Fortunately, I know where to drop him and I don't really need the company. That would interfere with dreaming of Peter.

Yeah, I'm nuts. He's headed to a toney college in a few weeks and I'm going to be sweating my ass off in Joffrey's training troop. I'm not looking for a long-term boyfriend. He probably isn't either. We could have some fun together and he can certainly afford to treat a girl right. And it seems like he might want to do that to dispel some rumors about him.

Peter's every girl's idea of gorgeous, but he's either secretly shy, sexually repressed, or gay. I don't read "gay" from his interactions with me – not even gay in the closet – but that's not what some other girls say. Until Tansy Collier started singing his sexual praises last spring, he really kept the rest of us guessing. My guess is he's shy or has high standards and that explains why he doesn't have a lot of second dates. I figure I have until his party to convince him that we can have fun for a couple of weeks before we go our separate ways.

Now I have to decide how best to approach him.

"Earth to Cheyenne," Josh says. "You just blew by the music store."

I blink and stare around me. Yeah, I wasn't paying attention. I swing around the block and drop him off, all the time weighing my options. Do I text him, call him, or just hope he drops Alyse off and I catch him again? I glance at the dash clock. I'm already late to be back to the studio when he would be dropping off Alyse. I'm not on the schedule for the front desk and my dance class isn't until tomorrow. I can't justify hanging around the studio. I'll look too eager and I sense that is not a good way to approach a guy who can have any girl he wants.

Wise Advice

Peter

Cheyenne's not at the studio when I drop off Alyse, so I head over to the marina to gas up the speed boat. Port Mallory's harbor isn't lovely. It's crowded with fishing boats and pleasure craft and there's a huge ferry terminal at one end. The Bay outside the breakwater is gorgeous and one of my favorite places in the entire world, but if you're standing on my boat next to the fuel fill-up, it's not an inspiring start for the day.

Captain Russell casts a big shadow, so I know it's him before I look over my shoulder. The man is massive. I'm over six foot, but he's maybe five inches taller than me with shoulders like a linebacker and the hard body of a man who works a physical job. He wears a baseball cap over his curls.

"Welcome back," the boatman says. He rents slips to pleasure craft and maintains half the harbor's hulls. My father keeps the yacht in one of his berths. I guess that's how he knows my comings and goings. "How was Europe?"

"Lots of old buildings. You ever been?"

"Took my wife to Venice a couple of years ago. For a boatman, it was a busman's holiday."

"What does that mean? I mean, I know it means it was all very familiar, but what does it refer to?"

"God, you're young!" He's used to me. We get along pretty good until I do something dumb, which is pretty frequent. Not this summer, though, because I've been away. "Back in the old days – as in mid-20th-century -- people took their vacations on Greyhound buses instead of planes or driving. So, for a bus driver, it would all be very familiar and he wouldn't feel like he got a vacation. I kept wanting to diagnose hull problems the whole time."

"Thanks." I spent a single day and two nights in Venice. I can guess there were a lot of hulls for him to diagnose. I like language. I want to understand it. Most people look at me like I'm crazy when I ask questions like that. Captain Russell drops to his haunches and watches what I'm doing. I brace for the lecture. There's *always* a lecture.

"Where you headed?"

"Out the Bay. Maybe that island with the old house on it."

"Maybe? That's kind of far out when you're going by yourself. When are you going to be back?"

"Before sunset. I gotta pick up my sister at dance at five o'clock." It's already 1:45.

"And you're going alone?" What is it with adults? I've done this hundreds of times. I don't need his guidance.

"Ben's working and I just sort of had this idea this morning."

"You shouldn't go out by yourself."

I peel my dry tongue off the roof of my mouth and stare out across the sun-reflective water.

"I won't go past the island."

"Does your radio work?"

Okay, good question. I turn it on. It's got power. I fiddle with the dial until I pull in the harbormaster.

"You file a float plan?"

"Not yet. I don't even know where I'm going." I sound irritable. My head's starting to hurt.

"Pete, your father would mobilize the National Guard if you disappeared. Don't end up on CNN."

Uh, yeah. Hadn't thought of that. That would probably run with the fountain footage. I stare at the Paul Bunyan-sized boatman and consider my options. Adults always seem to think I need direction and guidance. I spent nearly two months in Europe without adult supervision and I did just fine. Okay, except for that stupid fountain. But for heaven sake's, Ben and I sailed all over this bay since we were 11 years old and we're both still alive.

"Okay. I won't go out past the island and I'll stay to the east of it. Yeah, okay?"

"Still a huge area to search. Your transponder turned on?"

I look, snapping it on.

"Aye, aye, Captain."

"You think we're being overly concerned, but some of us grouchy old men want you to live to be a grouchy old man yourself. So, file a float plan before you leave. And, Pete, I know you're part-dolphin, but stay in the damn boat unless you've got someone with you."

"Yes, sir." I can swim from the island. He's right about the boat. Depending on the wave conditions, it can be hard to get back in. I swing up onto the dock.

"Where you going?" I'm confusing him, doing something unexpected.

"Forgot my water bottle and a hat."

I want to show him that I'm not irresponsible. See, I care about skin cancer ... kind of. I don't burn often, but the double exposure of the sun on the water and the fact that I didn't spend all summer in the sun means I need to be a bit more careful than usual. I pause at a tap to top off the water bottle.

It's a beautiful blue-and-gold day with fluffy white clouds way out to sea. The water ripples like a lake in a slight breeze. As soon as I clear the breakwater, I step up the throttle. I'm trying to imagine taking my European trip via bus. I've ridden busses for dance and school trips. Would it have been more restful than trains? I felt sick on at least half of them and I don't remember ever feeling like barfing on a bus.

Soon I'm approaching my destination. Built in the Roaring 20s, Cormorant Island House stands at the mouth of Mallory Bay, fortunately far enough to the east that it wouldn't become part of the proposed Long Island Bridge. Abandoned by the owner's business failure back in the dot.com collapse, the island estate stands forlorn and unkempt, about three acres of natural beauty with a beautiful four-story Victorian with craftsman features as the centerpiece. I haven't been here since last fall and a winter storm must have taken out the dock, leaving behind a pile of toothpicks. I rarely use the dock anyway because I don't like advertising that I'm trespassing. There's a little cove around the backside of the island that is perfect for my speed boat and there's a footpath that leads up to the actual grounds.

I always feel like I've stepped back into the past when I'm here. It's like I should wear a zoot suit and chaps as I imagine the partiers of Prohibition did. I'm dressed in jeans and an Oxford shirt. I strip to my birthday suit and swim around the little cove to cool off, then sit on a towel on the shore sipping my weak cocktail from the water bottle. I check my phone. I've got time. I find a pair of board shorts in the storage compartment under the boat's backseat and don my undershirt and tennis shoes to hike up to the house.

The footpath's been largely taken over by nature, so I have to take my time as I climb through seacoast scrub. About halfway up, the scrub grows among mature trees I assume were planted by the original owners. Abandoned about 20 years, the estate's starting to show the neglect. The glass on the greenhouse has been broken by storm-tossed branches. Seasons of leaves pile up on the porch. I peek through the few windows that haven't been boarded up. Dust covers provide a ghostly air to bare wood floors covered in layers of dust. So far there's no sign the elements have entered the house, but the trustees ought to pay better attention to their investment. The last I heard, the island boasted an asking price of $11 million, but all it would take is a tree limb through the roof during a storm and the price would plummet. I like architecture. That's why I care.

Or maybe it's because my uncle Matthew looked into buying it before he got sick the last time. I brought him out with my sailboat two years ago.

Remembering how excited he'd been by the property, the bourbon turns to acid in my mouth and I spit it out. He was sober that day – sober for a while – and starting to enjoy life again. He texted me a few weeks after heading home to say he'd put in an offer on the place. And, then he fell off the wagon and spiraled down pretty quickly. A couple of weeks before his death, he texted me all this delusional bullshit about how drinking will kill you. Yeah, he'd had Hep C, but it had been cured 10 years ago. Drinking on a compromised liver can kill you. I wipe tears as I dump out the water bottle. There's a tap by the greenhouse that still provides fresh water. I refill it and drink my fill.

The sun sparkles across the bay. Far out to the north, I see the Cross-Sound ferry with clouds starting to pile up behind it. My phone says I have lots of time, but the speedboat doesn't have an awning and I don't want to get involuntarily wet. I head back to the cove. I pause on the strand, looking toward the Mt. Calamity headland. I can see a good-sized yacht moored there. I wonder if I could swim that far. If the tide was with me, yeah, but it would make me late for picking up Alyse and then I'd have to get some help retrieving my boat.

The sun shimmers off the incoming waves, dazzling my eyes as I near the breakwater. Someday, I should sleep on the island and enjoy the peace as Matthew and I had dreamed of doing. For now, I have places to be and schedules to keep.

Talk with Mom

Ben

I come out of the shower and nearly run my mother down as she lugs a laundry basket toward the master bedroom. We both flinch and then laugh.

"I didn't think you were here." I relieve her of the basket of quilts.

"I was over at the Carsons letting a man view it. I'd forgotten that Greta said she'd left a basket of quilts for us."

Mom is acting on their behalf until their real estate agent can start next week.

"These are pretty." I don't know anything about quilting, but Greta Carson is apparently legendary for her quilts and I like the contrasting colors. I'm more interested in our potential new neighbors than our old ones. "Nice guy?"

"Seems to be. His son is in long-term care at Cedar Sinai, so he's moving his family here from Boston and is looking to buy."

"Wow, that's – cancer?" It's got to be serious to relocate so far.

"He didn't say, but he seemed pleased by that ramp out back, so I think it might be some sort of disability. Anyway, he took some photos, said he'd send them to his wife."

"That's fast, if they actually sell it, right?"

"It is."

I put the basket on the chair by the window.

"How are you doing?" My parents do actually care about how I'm doing.

"Fine. Going out with Pamela tonight." Mom knows we're not serious.

"You and Peter aren't getting together?"

"Nah, he's still jetlagged."

"Would you and Pamela like to come to the concert tomorrow night?"

"Not my thing anymore. King and Country are great musicians, but I'm not the church kid I used to be."

"I've noticed that. I guess I should just ask. Is your faith real to you any longer?"

"I don't know. I've just become – skeptical, I guess. I still believe, but I have doubts."

"We all have doubts."

"Do you? It doesn't seem like it."

"I've had a lot of seasons of doubt to work through where I am today. I won't get bossy with you, but I'll be praying that God makes Himself real to you. And, to Peter, because I think that boy really needs His guidance."

"Yeah, something's up with him, but I don't know what."

"He's not talking to you?"

"Pete's always kept secrets, Mom. You know that."

"Yeah, like why he was suspended from school and had to leave for a semester?"

I seldom remember that missing semester because it's been three years since Pete came back. If I'm honest with myself, it was a watershed. The Pete who came home is not the Pete I grew up with.

"He's never really explained that to me." That's not entirely true. I know he was caught on school grounds with pot, which seems unlikely since I know for sure he smoked pot for the first and only time last year. He didn't like it. So why would he be carrying pot on school grounds two, almost three years before he even tried it? Something is missing from his story. He's always kept secrets, but this feels different – almost like he's keeping someone else's secret. The secrets Pete keeps have to do with his mom. I can get him to talk about just about any other topic, though he's sometimes reluctant, but his mom gets his hackles up, so I gave up trying years ago. Mom sighs.

"What do you know that you're not telling me?"

What do I know? Not that much because Pete is good at hiding what bothers him. Besides, breaking his confidences isn't a good way to encourage him to confide in me.

"Maybe it's just that we spent the summer apart and we're about to go to different schools. He's more to himself than normal."

"Did something happen in Europe?"

"Not that he's mentioned."

If the folks don't know about the video, I'm not going to widen their horizons. Pete doesn't need to be more embarrassed than he already is. Right? It's not going to help to bring the adults into this. They don't have power over him anyway. His father is the only one who can … can … can what? When was the last time Alan Wyngate made a decision in Pete's life? It seems like he's been mostly calling his own shots since he was 15. Meanwhile, if my parents insisted they have input into one of my decisions right now – I turned 18 last month, but I'd still listen to them, though maybe I'd do what I want regardless. Does Governor Wyngate know what's going on in Pete's life or does he just not care?

"I need to go check on dinner." Mom moves to the door. I don't hang out in my parents' bedroom without one of them there, so I follow her, turning aside into my bedroom. My phone is blinking.

PAMELA - Great for getting together tonight. McCafferty's? I'd prefer if you didn't invite Peter. I know he's your best friend, but I don't like him.

I've never had a girlfriend dislike Pete. They usually like him more than they like me. Some of the things she's told me, though ….

I hate gossip, but a lot of the gossip she shared with me is stuff that's been going on for years and I just never noticed it. Does Pete know? I doubt it. Should he? Now there's a big question.

BEN – McCafferty's at 7:30 then. Meet you there.

Sigh. Another evening at the coffee shop. I so need to find something else to do with her, but that's one reason why we aren't serious.

All Kinds of Wrong

Peter

I'm feeling mussy by the time I'm back on land because it's like 3 am for me, so when Alyse flings me an irritated look when I stand at the observation window a few minutes before five, she tempts me to leave her ass right there. What the hell is her problem?

Maybe she knew the lecture was coming. Mrs. Sims hails from England and she's been teaching ballet for decades. I think she taught my mother. She's lecturing Alyse about tardiness as I walk up. For her, dance is all about discipline that extends way beyond the floor.

"Totally my fault, Mrs. S," I say. "My dad wanted to know how my trip to Europe was and I forgot I was giving Alyse a ride."

They always buy my lies. I keep expecting to get caught someday because I don't think I'm that good of a liar, but Mrs. Sims tells Alyse she can go put on her street clothes now, then places a motherly hand on my arm.

"I'm sorry I was late," Alyse murmurs before making her escape.

"Good that you see that, Miss Wyngate. I would love to give you more responsible roles, but dance requires discipline and not just on the dance floor." Translated – if you want that role in *Babes in Toyland* this winter, don't be late to class anymore.

"Yes, Mrs. Sims."

"Ah, and here is the wayward brother." We hug. She seems shorter than I remember. Why does Alyse look annoyed? What the heck?

"How are you, my dear?" Mrs. Sims taught me for years. She still had some dark in her hair when I started.

"I'm great. How are you?"

"Getting old." Mrs. Sims twinkles as she says this. I can see why her first dance role was as the Imp of Mischief in a Birmingham stage production. "Rebecca is taking on more and more duties. I'm just doing a few now – still tap, though."

"Of course. DTPM wouldn't be the same without your tap classes."

"Now if I could just get you to return to dance."

"Can't. I go to Yale in a few weeks."

"Pity. There are some fine dance companies in Hartford and Yale even has some dance classes."

"And, I'll give it some thought."

I won't. I saw that Yale has technique classes and I didn't sign up. The boarding school bullies teased me mercilessly until I find no joy in formal dance today. I'm not ever sharing that with Mrs. Sims or anyone else. Even Alyse doesn't know my reasons.

"How's your husband? Still working for DOT?"

"John is fine. And, yes, he retires next year. Rebecca and I are working on setting up a board so the studio continues."

"Lovely. I bet my dad would be glad to fund that."

"Oh, he's always been supportive of us. It's nice talking with you."

Alyse stows all her gear in her dance bag and heads for the door.

"I guess we're going." I chase after her, my mood deteriorating as I go.

"What is your problem?"

"Does it occur to you that my legs are tired and I'm hungry?"

"Try eating some real food. That might help."

"You're mean!"

"No. I'm just not obsessed with perfection. Get in the car. I want to get home too."

"Not so long as you could talk with Mrs. Sims."

"What is your problem? Seriously?"

Alyse slams the car door and turns her face into the window, fuming all the way to the house. I drive in silence, shooting surreptitious glances at her, but not apologizing for what I said. Mrs. Sims and I are old friends. What the hell is wrong with Alyse? When we get to the house, she bursts into tears and runs upstairs, slamming doors all the way. She makes so much noise Tilly comes out to the foyer with a questioning look on her face.

"Girls!" I snap. She laughs which just confuses me. Maybe you have to be a girl to understand girls. I'm in trouble if that's true. When I head upstairs, I have to walk by Alyse's bedroom to get to my own. Do I smell pot? I don't toke and it worries me that she does, but after I change into pajama bottoms and a t-shirt, I tap on her door. She doesn't answer me, so I try the knob. She's in the shower, so I sit down on the window seat, leaning my forehead on the glass and staring down at the rose garden. The room smells like she toked before she got into the shower.

The evening creeps in on silent cat's paws. She's not shocked to see me there when she comes out. Am I that predictable?

"I don't know why you're mad at me and I hate that you are. So how about you tell me what I've done wrong so I can stop?

Alyse smiles, as mellow as a cat on nip – or a teenager on pot.

"Why do you like her?"

"Mrs. Sims?"

"No, silly. Cheyenne?"

"Why not? She's pretty and I'm not looking for a long-term thing. I could hang out with her for a few weeks and then head off to Yale and probably never see her again."

"Except I dance with her." Alyse sits down on the other end of the daybed. Her sapphire blue silk robe opens a little too low for my comfort. I swallow tightly and turn my gaze out the window again.

"What does that matter? You two already don't like each other. Can't see that's going to change."

"But I'll have to pretend to like her."

"Why? I wouldn't pretend to like a boyfriend of yours that I didn't like."

"Wouldn't you?"

Nope, definitely not. I'd just ignore him, kind of like I'm ignoring the pot still lingering in the air.

"Do you really like her?"

"Not that much, but hanging out with her might be fun."

"Why don't you just hang out with me?"

"Is that what this is about -- you're afraid I won't spend time with you?"

"You're going away to college and leaving me here."

"Yeah. Kind of like when I went to boarding school."

"You still blame me for that, don't you?"

"No." I could have stopped it anytime by telling that lawyer that it was Alyse's pot. He knew it and he would have told Dad and things would have been different. "I chose to take the fall so you didn't have to."

"Why?"

Because I didn't know the consequences to my life, but I can't say that. What I do say is also true, just not as true.

"Because I love you and I didn't want to see you hurt."

"You're a great big brother."

"And you're high, so probably you should just mellow out, get some sleep. I'm still on European time so I'm going to crash too."

"Poor Tilly, making dinner for us and we don't even eat it."

73

"It's some sort of pasta dish so there will be great leftovers. I'm going to be--."

Alyse kisses me, cutting off my speech mid-word. Something comes to attention and I pull back, putting space between us.

"This isn't --. I'm --. Yeah." I leap up and run out of the room. What the hell?

What We Don't Say

Ben

Pete has wonderful taste and he's not ostentatious. He buys his ordinary clothes at outlets. He buys amazing leather goods that nobody would know cost more than I earn in a day at Temple. The wallet is butter soft in a rich saddle brown and I'm worried because he's not enjoying showing me the features. He pulls out the reddish hued match he bought himself so I can see how he set his up. That's so unlike Pete that I have to ask.

"You feeling okay?"

We're sitting in my room in the evening and he's blinking at the lamplight spilling across the plaid bedspread. His pupils look restricted and his forehead puckers.

"I think it's jetlag. Kind of have a headache."

I've seen Pete in all stages of messed-up over the last couple of years, but I'm not getting that read on him now. He smells of soap and sea air, just like he should smell after going to Cormorant Island. He's meeting my gaze, but not so much that I feel like he's lying. But there's something – I don't know.

"The coolest part is it's RFID protected, so you don't have to worry about your cards being scanned."

"Well, that's good. It really matters when you run everything out of your checking account. What's this weird pocket?"

"It's for Euros."

"*That* should come in handy." I roll my eyes and Pete grins, but he's definitely flagging tonight. "I've got a couple of days off next week while they retool the production line. Can we do Laurel Ridge?"

"Sure. It might take me a few days to get on this time zone. I didn't sleep much last night – kept waking up feeling like I was on a train."

"You mentioned those Euro trains travel really fast."

"They do and for some reason, that messed with my equilibrium."

"You never get motion sick." We laugh about a time when we all did a voyage on Hil Cavanaugh's yacht and the weather got rough. Pete had to bring us into port solo because he was the only one not puking.

"And I didn't get sick at first. Started in Munich, I think. Not getting enough sleep maybe."

Traveling on a hangover might have something to do with it too, but I don't say that.

"You okay? Something bothering you?"

"Other than jetlag? Alyse is just super emotional since I got back."

"It was a rough summer for her. She felt abandoned."

"Yeah, well, I'm going to college in a couple of weeks. She needs to get over it."

"She can travel up to see you – talk with you on the phone. Your phone was turned off most of the time you were in Europe."

"I told you why that was."

And, I want to believe him. I could believe he might ignore my calls if he was hungover or feeling motion sick on a train, but Alyse --. That's just not the relationship I've ever seen between the two.

"Hey, do you know Cheyenne?" He's changing the subject and that's more like Pete.

"I know a couple of Cheyennes. Last name?"

Pete opens his phone.

"Theriault?" He pronounces it the French way. (Terry-oh). I correct him. (Terry-alt)

"Her dad and my dad are friends through the Rotary. I think we've had classes together. You don't remember her?"

"From dance. I ran into her today at Dance Theater. What's she like?"

"Good sense of humor likes to party some. New guy every couple of months."

"Well, that's good since I'm headed to college."

"Yeah. I don't think she's looking for the love of her life just yet." He stares at the wall, unfocused for a moment. "Something is bothering you, isn't it?"

"Like I said, jetlag. I should head home, try to crash for the night. Maybe tomorrow I'll feel like I'm starting to sync with everybody else again."

I hesitate as he stands.

"You need me to drive you home?" It'll make me late to meet Pam, but he's making me nervous.

"Naw. I'm good. I'll just ride with the windows down. Your birthday present is on its way. I didn't find what I wanted until we were in London, so it's in the mail."

"I'm fine even if you forgot."

"I didn't. Just can't make the British and American posts work faster. Good night."

I watch him from the window as he walks to his car. He pauses, looks at the sky and breathes a heavy sigh. Something's wrong, but I don't know what, and it feels like a big fishhook pulls my guts behind his car as he drives away.

Party Planning

Peter

Trevor's phone goes to voice mail. Suppressing an impatient growl, I ignore his message while formulating my own.

> **PETER - I'm booking the food and drink now. Hope you'll DJ. My house, Friday next, 7:00 pm? Let me know.**

I stare at the webpage where my order of food and drink await. Am I absolutely sure I want to do this on a Friday rather than a Saturday? Alyse has a dance thing that evening, which means Trevor and Cheyenne might also. Yeah, maybe Saturday would be better. Friday suits me because Dad is less likely to show up in the middle of things, but if Saturday works better for everyone else ....

My phone vibrates across the desktop. I enter my lock-screen code to talk with Trevor.

"I've got a dance thing Friday."

"I remembered that about two seconds after I hit SEND. So I'll order the caterer for Saturday."

"Can you tap the new microbrewery – Carlman's?" Trevor's languid drawl suggests he's just smoked a bowl. How can he accomplish anything in a constant state of intoxication? I haven't had a drink since the island and I'm starting to enjoy the clarity.

I sweep the computer screen.

"Yeah, I'll get a keg. Can you get here around five for set up?"

"No problem. I got a new honey."

"Yeah?" My gut tightens, thinking he might mean Cheyenne.

"Macaria Berber."

"I know her?"

"Yeah. You dated her for about two seconds in 8th grade."

"That seriously does not ring a bell."

"I'll text a photo to you. I think you took her to a movie or something."

After a moment's silence, my phone vibrates and I pull it away from my ear to look at the photo – messy dark hair, laughing blue eyes with more lines than an 18-year-old should have.

"We didn't date. We just went to an assembly together. She still smoking?"

"Hot? Yeah!"

"No, cigarettes? That's why I never asked her out. Her breath stank."

"I don't care about her breath. It'll be smelling of ganga anyway."

"Your choice, man. How do you feel about watermelon?"

"Filled with vodka?"

"No, to eat."

"Yeah, filled with vodka. Seriously, man, you got this. I gotta go. My mom wants me to drive my brother to soccer practice."

Trevor doesn't sound drive-ready, but it's not any of my business, so I don't say anything. He hangs up. I complete the catering list and hit SEND. Then I text Cheyenne.

> PETER - Saturday at 7 pm
>
> CHEYENNE - Just like that?
>
> PETER - I've got a black belt in party planning.
>
> CHEYENNE - My parents would never allow it.
>
> PETER - Mine is never around to notice.
>
> CHEYENNE - Guess he's kind of busy.

She includes an emoji I don't know the meaning of. It looks like a little blue woman scratching her chin in thought.

I sigh. Nobody gets what it's like to be the *de facto* man of the house because my father is never here. The kiss Alyse laid on my mouth still lingers.

> **PETER** - *Looking forward to seeing you there. Maybe we could hang out.*

> **CHEYENNE** - Maybe. Is it a date?

> **PETER** - *Do you want it to be?*

> **CHEYENNE** - I wouldn't object.

> **PETER** - *Then yeah.*

I'm swelling again, so set the phone down to adjust my clothing. A knock taps on the door. I locked it against Alyse, so I have to get up to open it. I tell Cheyenne I'll get back with her.

"Keeping secrets?" Tilly asks.

"More like privacy. Alyse needs to learn to knock." I gesture for her to come in.

"Good luck with that." Tilly sits down on my love seat while I close the door. "What's with the huge liquor order?" The catering app must notify her phone.

"I want to have a party next Saturday." She's never questioned these purchases before. My heart thumps.

"Okay. That's fine, but I don't want a repeat of graduation weekend."

Absolutely. That was dumb.

"It won't be."

"It almost ended up badly."

"I know. I'm sorry. It won't happen again. Besides, this is my last party. I doubt we'll all get together after we go off for school."

Tilly sighs.

"Growing up is hard." I know nothing of her childhood. Was hers hard? "And the fishbowl of your father's life is harder. Promise me you won't drink too much this time."

"Yeah. No, I don't know what happened that night, but it won't happen again. I promise. I didn't mean to scare you."

"That doctor – Schaefer – he said you had a problem."

"I don't. I just tried to prove something to someone and it got out of hand. I learned my lesson."

I tried to drink Finn Conover under the table and discovered Finn has two hollow legs. I think I won, but when I woke up in the ER after having my stomach pumped, it didn't feel like a victory.

"Good. I'll let you have one last party, but it better not end up in the emergency room again. I might not be able to keep it a secret from your father again."

I repeat my promise and she smiles. Tilly always has my back. I trust her most of the time.

"Are you going to tell me the real reason your door was locked?" She knows me so well.

"I did. Alyse barges in when she wants and she didn't stop when I told her, so I locked the door."

"I took her to dance hours ago." I know that. I was awake when Tilly's car backed out of the driveway. My sleep schedule is taking a long tour of time zones and is currently halfway between Europe and Long Island. Maybe by next Saturday, I'll be aligned with everyone else. A guy can hope anyway.

"I seriously wasn't locking you out."

"Then what were you doing? You knew she wasn't home."

I sigh and my anatomy responds to the memory of Alyse's taste on my lips. I surreptitiously pull a pillow onto my lap, but I'm not subtle enough. Tilly's eyebrow raises.

"Wow," she murmurs. "I didn't see that coming."

"Nothing's coming. I didn't – she's my sister."

Tilly nods. This conversation is more awkward than having my sister's taste on my lips.

"Anyway. Nothing's going to happen. We just --. Stupid. And I don't want to talk about it."

Tilly's mouth tightens. She takes a deep slow breath and lets it out twice as slowly.

"She's a lot like your mother."

Alyse does look like Laren. So do I, though my hair is curly – a gift from my paternal grandfather. Alyse and I both resemble her. Tilly's looking in my face and I don't know what she wants. Maybe my agreement.

"She does look like her."

"That's --." She sighs, looks away from me, and starts again. "That's not what I mean." She heaves a deep breath again. "There are some things we can't talk about. But I hope you have someone to talk to."

I nod. Tilly gets up, leaving me to stare out the window.

My mom is gorgeous! She isn't just beautiful. Black hair and cornflower blue eyes, still a great figure after four kids. Even cameras think she's lovely. But it's more. She glows with this energy. That's the bipolar. I figured that out last summer when I went to visit her. It cast my childhood in a different light. It was like she lit the room just for me. I'd do anything for her attention, to be warmed by her solar flares. But it was so – changeable. One minute I was flying and the next I was buried under a ton of shit. When Laren crashes, it's a fall off a cliff into blackest drowning water. Sun bright and darkest black and nothing in between.

The kids she has with Sam have him, but my dad wasn't around much and I can imagine Tilly didn't speak up for us then like she does now. I spent my childhood on that rollercoaster. I know bipolar better than if I had it myself.

Does Alyse remind me of her? She's like Laren without the extremes ... mostly. Yesterday's outburst felt a little like Mom. Alyse's brights are not all-consuming and her darks are brief and there's a between. Or do I have to believe that?

My head's buzzing and my thoughts ping around like a pinball. My neck tightens and my stomach clenches. I dissipate my tension with a two-chug draw on the bottle of bourbon. While I'm enjoying the spreading warmth, I see Tilly's BMW pull out from the garage. The clock says it's 4:30. I should be getting Alyse. Why didn't Tilly remind me? I've spent all day in my room and I'm still wearing my pajamas when it's a gorgeous summer's day outside. What is wrong with me?

Spoiled Brats

Cheyenne

Alyse Wyngate is a spoiled rotten rich girl and I struggle to see her brother in her. Yeah, they look alike – both slender and tall with black hair. His eyes are green and hers are blue – both enormous in slim faces. You can see they're related, but his bone structure is stronger, rendering his face in sharp angles and plains. She looks delicate, but she is like a Siamese cat – lithe and vicious.

She knows it too. She plays that delicacy to its highest string and then wraps it around your throat like a garrote. Believe me. I know rich kids. There are a lot of them in Port Mallory. Most of them go to private school, but they still attend Dance Theater or something else, so we rub shoulders now and then. Most of them think they're better than the rest of us. They casually flaunt their wealth in our faces and then are shocked when we don't bow before them like the royalty they think they are. That's Alyse too.

Alyse has the best of everything. One of her leotards costs more than all of mine. She's got custom toe shoes. Everything she wears has either a designer label or none – which is a sure sign it cost more than my allowance for a month. I wonder what happens to all that crap when she's outgrown it.

Pete's always gone to public school, which might explain why he's more regular people. He's got a hot car, but he wears ordinary clothes and he doesn't complain about schlepping coffee from Starbucks. He's generous with his blessings too, willing to open his wallet instead of pretending he can't afford it or pitch in instead of acting like he'll melt if he has to work a little. Truthfully, Trevor's that way too. They both come from money but join in the car washes and other fund-raisers needed to keep DTPM open. Pete's even helped out a few times since he's quit dancing. Most rich people's kids are not that giving.

But it's more than that. I remember Pete giving tap shoes to a financially strapped younger student. It had been so classy – the shoes in the kid's locker with a note saying "I outgrew these and they look to be about your size." And, they weren't the highest quality, designer shoes that would make the kid look like a charity case. They were ordinary, just like what the rest of us wore. Had Pete ever worn them? Who knew? I was impressed that he knew not to make the kid look bad. Kip is now graduating into the senior company. He'll take Trevor's place when Trevor leaves for Joffrey next month. Like me, he covers the front desk sometimes to offset the cost of classes and dance gear.

I'm thinking all this as I dance the ballet-jazz fusion piece. Alyse's performance is flawless. She's going to move up because I'm leaving and she's that talented, but I hate her. I truly loath her because she is soulless. Her flawless performance means nothing without anything motivating it.

A woman greets her when we exit the class. I'm surprised to see they look nothing alike until I remember Pete doesn't have a mother. Or, er…he has a mother who is absent. This must be the infamous Tilly he's mentioned. She's not their step-mother, but she seems motherly. Alyse's attitude is rude and whiny. Pete put up with it too the other day. They're teaching her to get away with it.

I'm supposed to pick up my younger brother and take him home before I come back for the evening intensive for the advanced company, so I go to the dressing room along with Alyse.

"I'll be out when I'm ready," Alyse snaps as she comes in through the door. I pause in snapping up my jeans and reach for my shirt. "God, she is *so* bossy."

Pete speaks fondly of Tilly, so I don't know what to say. She must read something in my expression.

"She's not my mother and she should know her place."

"As the one your father left in charge of you?"

She's got the same full lips that make Pete seem so kissable, but hers curl into a sneer as she rounds on me.

"What do you know? You know my brother is just entertaining himself until he goes to Yale, right?"

Yeah, I assumed that Pete is doing the same thing I'm doing – hanging out with someone entertaining until summer ends. But, what is it about rich kids who can't say "I'm going to college next week." No, instead they feel the need to name drop the institution they can afford to attend. I can do that too.

"And, I go to Joffrey at about the same time." I push up on pointe in my regular ballet slippers and pirouette out the door. Most ballerinas can't do on pointe unsupported, let alone manage to travel, but I've got strong feet. Let's see if she masters *that* by the time she graduates.

I drop to my soles and give Tilly a smile. She probably deserves it for putting up with Alyse. She smiles back, then arranges her face in a neutral expression as her duckling follows me into the lobby. I wonder if Pete has mentioned me to her. We only have a couple of weeks, so I doubt I'll ever know.

Cooler Heads

Peter

My grandparents' house in Old Field is enormous, but somehow it has a soul that ours lacks. Yes, you could fit three of our huge house in theirs, but you feel welcome. Comfortable. Not small or unwanted. It's surrounded by rich green lawns, broken by well-groomed groups of trees, graced with a pond and a pool and with this terrific view of the ocean. We don't have a pool because my mother preferred roses, which she didn't take with her when she left. She took the piano which I played, but not the roses that I hate. Every time I see them, I am reminded of that bedroom and Sam's surprised look.

Rather than wander the halls trying to find my grandfather, I stroll around the wide terraces to the conservatory where he spends most of his time now that he's semi-retired. Retirement wouldn't suit him. He's too alive to sit down and rest. Instead, he made uncle Adam his CEO and he works three days a week from an office here and commutes into Manhattan when it suits him. My grandmother Lucy still runs a non-profit from another office here on the estate. They seem happy.

Bosco the chocolate Lab accompanies me during much of my journey, carrying his battered retrieving dummy and wagging his tail like a propeller, clearly asking for me to send it sailing as far across the lawn as I can. Just as we reach the doors to the conservatory, I grant his wish and then slip inside.

The glass doors are open to catch the breezes, the screened doors keeping the bugs out. My grandfather sits on a rattan couch, his bare feet up on a matching table, a book open on his lap. He looks at me and removes his reading glasses. He sets them atop his bookmarked novel and rises to give me a hug. That always feels awkward because my dad is not a hugger. I wonder that Michael Peter Wyngate is reading *Girl on Fire*. He's always had a love of science fiction and he forced me to read Bradbury and Heinlein, but somehow I didn't expect him to like modern authors.

"Must I ask you how your trip was, or will you tell me what you wished you'd had time to do?"

He knows me so well.

"A week in Italy wasn't enough. I should have gone to Greece and Scandinavia. I wanted to hike the Alps. I could spend a year studying the architecture of about five of the cities I didn't spend enough time in."

Granddad Mike smiles at me. He's still got his hair and he's stopped straightening it, so it's a mass of curls that remind me of hobbits.

"Want to go for a walk?"

Again, he knows me. I hate the humidity of the conservatory, especially this late in the afternoon. It's fine in the winter, but in the summer, it's just too close even with the fans that circulate in the high ceiling.

Bosco comes as soon as we step out the door. Granddad tosses the dummy for the dummy. I laugh at my pun.

"Amusing yourself?"

"It's funnier in my head."

"Just remember – musing is thinking – a-musement is not thinking."

He's where I get my interest in language from. Although I ought to be annoyed that he's telling me to think, I file away the bit of language trivia to google later. We walk toward the pond. It's his favorite spot on the property which is perhaps the most peaceful place I know.

"What did you think of Austria?"

"It's beautiful. Didn't get to spend much time there – two days one night in Vienna."

"Too bad. I spent a year there between high school and college."

"Your parents let you take a gap year?" I remember my great-grandfather who passed about five years ago. My great-grandmother lives in a penthouse with a view of Central Park. She laughed when she caught me skateboarding in her foyer, which is the size of an Olympic swimming pool. She asked me if I would teach her and then after I showed her what I could do, she said she'd have to buy some safety gear so she wouldn't hurt herself. The box came as a gift box a few days later with a hand-written note saying "I really like your brain, elbows, and knees. Maybe you'd humor me by protecting them." If I still skateboarded, I'd probably need larger pads now. Would I use them? I don't know.

"We called it 'dropping out' in those days. They weren't happy about it, but when I didn't come back from my summer tour, they didn't have a lot of choice. My father cut off my allowance thinking they'd get me home again. That was a shock, standing there in the American Express office being told there were no funds available, but I took a job at a ski lodge in the Tyrols and stayed the winter. Made fast friends with the noble businessman who owned the resort. He hired me as a front desk clerk because I could speak English and German, but he ended up using me as a translator when he hosted this business meeting between an American firm and a German factory. I went home the next summer with some connections my father respected. I went to college and enjoyed four years of learning. Went back after graduation and bought a bit of land from my friend and built a chalet."

"Where my parents honeymooned?" He nods, smiling, then grimaces slightly. I know what he's thinking. She *hated* Austria. It was the first of many disappointments she occasionally airs about my father. "She's, uh, hard to please."

"Clearly. I don't wish to disparage your mother."

"She deserves it." Seriously, I don't think Laren ever loved Alan. Not that her family was poor, but his family was richer, so she snagged him at Yale and dragged him down into her turbulent death roll. Did I rescue him? I've never known for sure.

Granddad Mike squeezes my shoulder, throws the dummy for the dog, and then looks intently into my face. I can't meet his gaze.

"I am happy to see you, but I don't think you came to talk about your trip. What's wrong?"

I came all this way wanting to talk about it, but it isn't easy to just speak it out. I open, then close my mouth a half-dozen times before I figure out how to start it.

"Since I've gotten back – Alyse keeps acting like – like – uh – I'm her boyfriend."

He glances at me, throws the retrieving dummy into the pond, turns towards me.

"You two are unusually close."

"Yeah. Maybe weirdly close."

"She's jealous?"

I shake my head.

"Um, affectionate."

His blue eyes twitter and I catch of whiff of blown antiperspirant. I've scared him now, but he's a heroic grandfather. He's trying to figure out what to say and I want to help.

"Nothing's happened. She kissed me and I've been avoiding her ever since."

He rubs the back of his neck, watching Bosco chasing fish. Dogs are silly beasts.

"Have you told her how inappropriate that is?"

"I tried." I sigh. "I don't know what to do about it."

"No, it's hard. You love your sister, but – I hope you don't love her in that way." I feel my cheeks flush. "Of course you don't. You wouldn't bring it up if you did."

"That's true." I could boil water on my cheeks.

"Seventeen-year-old male bodies don't always follow their wiser heads, Peter."

I hadn't thought of that. My anatomy reacts to any expanse of female skin. I just didn't expect it to react to my sister's lips on mine.

"I'm embarrassed by it."

"Yeah. That's good. Given your mother's – should I even bring this up?"

"He told you?"

Granddad Mike looks uncomfortable. It's a messy topic and I don't want to talk about it, but he thinks he owes me an explanation.

"It was a mess, Peter. He needed someone to talk to. That's what fathers are for. If he weren't in Albany, you probably would have talked to him about Alyse."

Probably not. I can't imagine telling Alan about Alyse. I haven't told him much since I told him about Laren. My father thinks methodically until he gets his hackles up and then he tosses the whole world into chaos.

"Did he follow your advice?"

"Not really. I told him to divorce her and sue for custody. He gave her a choice instead and she chose to leave and not take you children with her."

"So you got what you advised anyway."

"It saved a battle in court, I suppose. He got lucky that she didn't want to fight. A battle might have required you to admit what happened between you."

"Nothing really happened. Touching."

He looks sad.

"Sure that's not just what you choose to remember?"

I'm not going there. I throw the dummy for Bosco. Granddad Mike rubs the back of his neck and lets the subject drop.

"You're off to Yale in a few weeks, yes?"

"Yeah."

"This whole episode with Alyse should end when you're in Connecticut. I'll ask Lucy to talk with her."

My heart starts beating in terror. My grandmother pulls no punches. Now that I've shared with Granddad it's impossible to stop what I've set in motion. It's kind of the story of my life.

"I should go. Thanks for talking."

"Any time, Peter. You do understand? None of this is your fault."

I shrug, though the truth is that I'm pretty sure my grandfather doesn't know the half of what is my fault.

Red Kryptonite

Ben

Pete's waiting across from my driveway when I get home from work. He looks exhausted, dark bruises under his eyes, as he leans against his car. I invite him into the house. Mom must have taken Wes somewhere and it's too early for Dad.

When I get out of the shower, Pete is sprawled on my carpet, his long legs taking up a lot of floor space, while he reads an old comic book.

"Which one is that?" I lower myself to the carpet.

"1958 – Red Kryptonite. I think I liked the Smallville version better."

"You *would* prefer an intoxicating kryptonite over one that makes you weaker than green kryptonite."

"So would you. I'm just honest about it." He's right and we laugh about it. It doesn't quite take the exhaustion from his face.

"Jetlag still got you mixed up?"

"Yeah, but you mentioned you have days off."

"I do and it just seems like we don't want to waste them."

"We don't. So what do you suggest?"

"How about Splish Splash?"

He's tired, so it takes a minute for him to warm to the idea.

"That sounds like fun. Weather report says it's going to be over 90 degrees tomorrow. What time?"

"When it opens – 10 am. I'll pick you up at 9:00 am."

He groans, but flashes his trademark Pete smile. He puts the comic back in its sleeve on the shelf with the others, then just sits there staring into space, arms crossed across his bent knees. He used to do that a lot the summer his mother left. I can't imagine my parents divorcing, so I didn't know how to help him. Plus we were 12 and what 12-year-old really knows what to say when their friend is hurting? Mostly we just read comic books, watched Smallville and drank way too much Mountain Dew. Eventually, Pete stopped being so sad. Or did he just learn to cover it up?

"What are you doing this evening?"

I'm supposed to meet Pamela at Walt Whitman in about an hour, but now I hesitate.

"You need to hang out?"

"I don't know. The house is too quiet and – I don't know."

"What's going on?"

"I just – I don't know. It just feels – I don't know."

"How much sleep did you get last night?"

"I kept waking up."

"Because you were planning your party?" I got the text invitation this afternoon.

"No, because I felt like I was on a train or a plane. It's like I can't settle down."

"You really sound – I don't know."

"That's my line."

He grins, but I'm not buying it.

"You know what I mean. What happened in Europe this summer?"

"Nothing. I'm just … I can't explain it."

He sounds down and certainly, I've seen him that way before. Pete needs activity like some people need air. It's not ADD. He can sit for hours so long as he's engaged, but he gets restless if there's nothing to concentrate on. Even sleeping over when we were kids, he needed music to keep from talking to me so we could sleep. The price of all that attention is he occasionally crashes and sleeps for a day or two to reset. He seems to be way beyond his usual exhaustion. It's like he's hung up on a wire, unable to relax.

"So maybe you should go home and sleep so you can have fun tomorrow."

"You have plans tonight?"

"They're flexible. Let's just go to – I don't know – how about we go downstairs and play ping-pong or to your place and play pool?"

"Yeah?" He sounds like it's a question, but then he responds with a stronger voice. "No. I don't want to see Alyse."

"Why?"

"It's complicated. But, yeah, ping pong. Just best out of three coz, you're right, I need sleep."

He beats me two out of three, which isn't surprising. He's got reach on me and his girlfriend wasn't lighting up his phone demanding to know why he canceled. Just as we finish, Pamela pulls up in the driveway. Her last message said everything about why.

PAMELA – Look, I know he's your friend, but he's manipulating you.

Pete flinches as she comes into the basement family room, but then he puts on the face he uses when he doesn't want anyone to know what he's thinking. It works on most people. Not me and probably not Alyse, but most people cannot see the turmoil behind the mask.

"Hi, Peter, how are you?"

He's not fooled by Pamela's bright tone. He's not said anything about trying to date her a few years ago. We kind of made a rule when we were in junior high that we would never date each other's exes, but they never dated. He hasn't mentioned that, and he's said not a disparaging word about Pam. I had kind of forgotten that she'd deeply wounded him when she turned him down. I might not have started dating her if I'd remembered.

"Hey, Pam. What are you up to?"

"Just trying to figure out why my boyfriend suddenly canceled on me."

I suddenly feel like the guy that accidentally farts aloud in the movie. I didn't tell Pete I had plans with Pamela. Pete slides a gaze my way.

"I guess he got a better offer." The mask's got a lazy smile as Pete gestures to the ping pong table.

Pamela's mouth tightens. She's a really sweet girl, a pastor's daughter, not given to the cattiness of some girls, and I'm surprised that she's thinking of going for Pete's jugular.

"We haven't hung out in months and he dropped by." I'm trying to quell the troubled waters, but Pamela's eyes flash in my direction.

"Canceling was kind of rude."

"I agree." What? He's on her side? Nope, but the mask sure is. "I'll see you tomorrow morning. You two should watch Netflix or something. Alyse said something about a new chick flick."

"Do you know which one?" Pamela asks. Her claws are still out.

"No. I don't watch chick flicks with my sister, but I'm sure you can find it. See you in the morning, Ben."

Pete heads for his car and leaves me and Pamela not looking at one another.

"You really don't see it, do you?" She's waited for Pete to drive away before speaking.

"See what?"

"How he uses people."

"No, I don't see that. He's my friend, and he's been gone all summer. So, yeah, we want to hang out with one another. And why do you think he's manipulating me?"

"I bet he came up with some reason for you to hang after he found out you were meeting me."

I can't really remember now.

"I think ping pong was my idea."

"Why?"

"He seemed down and – I just didn't think the mall sounded like fun."

"Apparently not as much fun as you plan on having tomorrow. What are you doing?"

"Splish Splash."

"Really?"

"Yeah, really. He and I have gone at least once a summer since we were old enough to reach the height bar."

"And maybe that's why you don't see who he has become."

"Maybe you've just never given him a chance. Maybe if you got to know him, you'd see what I see."

"Doubtful. Besides, summer's almost over. It's not like we have a lot of time to get to know each other."

"Why don't you come with us tomorrow?"

"Really?" I expected her to say no because she is so girly, but then she grins. "Yeah, that would be fun. It's been a couple of years, but water slides on a hot day – definitely worth the price. But you probably don't want him to feel like a third wheel."

"He's kind of interested in Cheyenne Theriault. Maybe I should suggest he invite her."

"Cheyenne, huh? Why not?"

"You know her?"

"Sure. We had classes."

"Nice girl?"

"Depends on the definition of 'nice'. She's polite enough, friendly, competitive. She's one of those girls who has sex with every guy she dates."

"I'll advise him to wear a condom."

"Really?"

"Can't hold Pete to standards he doesn't aspire to."

I'm texting him while she's talking. It takes a while before he texts me back.

PETER – Cheyenne has agreed to be my date. We're not telling Alyse, right?

Pamela reads the text.

"No, of course not. You wouldn't want your long-term girlfriend to interfere with your new short-term girlfriend."

I think about Alyse coming onto me this summer. Yeah, you could think it might just be a young girl trying out her feminine wiles, but I've been like a brother to her since before kindergarten. I think Pamela's wrong on that assessment.

"Can you just let that alone for now?" She's pretty when she frowns. "Just – they're really close, but I don't think Pete's – I just don't see that."

"Maybe you don't see it because you're not looking."

"Yeah, could be – but could you leave it alone tomorrow. Just let him enjoy his date. Maybe he'll surprise you if you give him time to show you he's not who you think he is."

Pamela shakes her head and then picks up one of the paddles.

"I can do that. I don't think I'm wrong, but I think you can figure it out without my nagging you." She hands me the other paddle. "Best two out of three?"

"Oh, you are on, tennis lady."

First Date

Peter

Splish Splash is a frenetic, bipolar kind of place – Lazy River and giant waterslides – a group kind of place. It was Ben's idea originally. It snowballed from there. Pamela found out about it and I think invited herself and suggested I bring a date. Big of her. So I called Cheyenne.

She's dressed for the water park – aqua bathing suit covered by a navy-blue quick-dry t-shirt, a pair of aqua-and-navy board shorts, and hot-pink reef-walkers. I always feel like I should treat everyone, but I've learned it makes people uncomfortable, so I don't offer. I just pay for me and Cheyenne. Ben wouldn't have suggested it if he didn't have the money.

Us men want to go to the big water slides. Yeah, there's the adrenaline rush of flying down a twisting slide on a thin

107

flow of water, but it's a lot better when you're doing it with a pretty girl between your legs. Multiply that by a couple dozen times and – yeah. Ben's a genius.

"I'm so sorry." Cheyenne truly looks concerned as I try to walk out the pain at the bottom of the flume.

"It's fine. I can limp for a few days. You're going to Joffrey. You can't hurt yourself and perform at that level."

"You're sweet. And you're right. Trevor told me not to bruise myself or he'll be going to Joffrey alone."

"Trevor's going to Joffrey too?"

"He is. You ever see him dance?"

"Yeah, he was the troll king to your angel."

"What night did you come?"

"The first Saturday."

"Oh, that's awful. I messed up so badly." She's laughing amid her wince. "Did she tell you about that?"

"Of course, she did." I sigh, laughing with her. "What *actually* happened?"

"I turned the wrong way at the start of a very technical movement. I needed to be somewhere else entirely to start the next section and I had no idea how to get there. He caught me, whispered 'trust me' in my ear and executed five lifts with flourishes to get us where we needed to be. I had no idea how he did it."

"He's a powerful dancer."

"You were supposed to dance that role, weren't you? You didn't know?"

"I thought you'd rechoreographed." I knew something had gone wrong, but neither of them let on, which is the essence of dance performance that I miss. It's performance art. There's no retakes. If you screw up, you cover and you do it beautifully with a smile on your face. If only life were so easy.

"I remember being very excited that you'd be my partner."

My cheeks warm at her compliment. I forgot that she'd been cast as the angel. We only practiced a few times before I got caught carrying Alyse's cannabis on school grounds. That got me shipped to boarding school and I never danced ballet again.

"Yeah." I sigh. I'm over it. "Can't say I could have rescued that performance like he did. Let's go find something less likely to bruise us."

"Lazy River?"

"If you don't mind. We can come back and do the slides when my glutes stop spasming."

She gives me this curious look and I have no idea what it means.

"What about Ben and Pam?"

"They'll figure it out." She's skeptical. I love her facial expressions. Subtle and yet utterly readable. "Last time we were here, Ben abandoned me for an hour while he went and found food to eat. I finally found him at Johnny Rockets eating a burger the size of my head."

She laughs, a throaty purr than makes my anatomy vibrate. I can't be like this in a public place. It's embarrassing. We pass a flock of girls who are clearly here to attract attention. Swimsuits cut up above their hipbones and barely restraining their breasts bother me, but the looks they cast me like I'm a piece of meat in a window at de Wallens are a major turn-off. Cheyenne studies my face as we walk.

"What?" I hate when girls check out my abs and below, but when they look intently into my face, I want to know what they're thinking.

"I'm just wondering why you invited me here."

"We said we wanted to go on a date. This is appropriately first-date-like. Right?"

She's still staring at me and it's becoming a problem because she can't stare at me *and* avoid running into passersby.

"Just ask whatever you're thinking." She's sat on my lap on a waterslide, so I don't feel shy about taking her arm to steer her through a crowd of what have got to be football players. You know, walking walls of muscle and testosterone. I bet there are physical feats I can do that they can't – or at least not for as long as I can do them. I once challenged Jess Norton, the captain of the football team, to stand on his toes for longer than me. First position demi-point – I outlasted him by five minutes and then did twenty releve to drive home the point that dancers are stronger than football players. That was before boarding school.

"You have a reputation."

"Doesn't everyone?" She gives that throaty laugh again, which makes me long for the water to hide in. "What is my reputation?"

"Sexy and self-absorbed."

"One-night-stand-Pete?"

"Easier to buy than the earlier ones that you were gay."

I didn't know that rumor until after it died the death it deserved. I just wondered why girls gave me a funny look when I asked them out. I know why the "gay" rumors went away. Tansy Collier and I got super-drunk near the end of spring semester junior year and she spread it all over the school that I took her virginity. I remember most details of that night and I'm pretty sure I'm still a virgin. It wasn't for want of trying that time, but alcohol … you know? And then she passed out just as the booze wore off some. There are lines I won't cross and sex with an unconscious chick is one of them.

"That was a function of being nearly a year younger than the rest of the class." My cheeks warm again.

"That's what Ben said when the rumors were circulating." I guess Ben is where I got the idea from. I remember being embarrassed that girls had me befuddled when most of my friends seemed to be getting laid. I'm not befuddled anymore. I just don't want to make a mistake I can't bribe or cajole my way out of. "I just see you get shy around girls."

"Maybe I'm not my reputation." She raises an eyebrow. Now I've done it and I'll need to explain. "Maybe I like to take my time and get to know people before I'm that intimate with them."

"Is that why you never have a second date?" She slides a teasing gaze my way.

"I have had second dates." I'm pretty sure I've had second dates. Francesca – the girl in Monaco – we went out five nights in a row. And there was … yeah, not a lot. The problem is that I usually get them drunk and they puke or pass out before I'm ready to do it. I usually lose interest after that. The ones that pass out make assumptions about what happened when they were out. You'd think a girl who thinks she's been taken advantage of would object, but apparently not if it means they can brag to their friends that they had sex with me. Thus, a virgin becomes a whore and I don't know how to overcome that reputation. It might help if when guys ask me for details, I answer directly, but – yeah, I prefer that reputation over the one that I'm gay. Maybe I shouldn't date girls who try to keep up with me drink for drink. I'm legendary and generally larger than most of the girls I would date. Maybe Macaria could outdrink me. Certainly in junior high, she could.

Cheyenne laughs. I'm not sure why and it doesn't matter because we've reached the Lazy River and there are innertubes to choose. I do the manly thing and lift her into her side before settling into mine. I've never brought a girl to Splish Splash before, so I hope this is okay and she isn't objecting. The attendant gives me a friendly nod as the current carries us away.

I like the Lazy River. It's peaceful after the big slides, especially when I can feel a deep bruise developing on my left buttocks. It reminds me a bit of sailing. I use my arms and legs as rudders to control our drift. Cheyenne announces she doesn't mind going under fountains and then breaks up laughing when I say "I can do fountains."

"I didn't mean that." My cheeks warm.

"It looked fun. Why are you embarrassed by it?"

"Because of who my dad is, everybody watched it."

I don't want to talk about it, so I spin us under a fountain. She throws up her arms and takes the water spill full in the face. I shake the water out of my hair to stop it running into my eyes. She's looking at me sideways with this big goofy grin on her face, so I aim for another fountain. Her t-shirt is clinging to her breasts and the water makes her summer tan glow like a peach glistens after a rain. I am

112

seized with a sudden urge to kiss her, and for once, I act on it.

I've kissed my share of girls, including Francesca in Monaco, and Cheyenne is among the best. She tastes of strawberries. Her lips are open slightly, offering access to my tongue if I want but not invading my mouth with hers without an open invitation.

I pull back to meet gazes and her eyes open just as we go under another fountain. We emerge laughing, floating backward

I drop my right arm into the current and direct us under another fountain. This time, I send us into the deep pocket under the ledge, leap off the two-seater and scoop her up in my arms and I'm not shy about where my tongue goes now. Standing in the hip-deep water, I don't have to worry about embarrassing myself. I don't know how much time we spend kissing. I'm eventually distracted by an innertube to the back.

"Wow," Cheyenne murmurs as a small child giggles and floats away.

"You like body surfing?"

"What? We were kissing."

"I don't want to be too pushy."

"Right." We kiss again. When we break, her breasts are heaving.

"Bodysurfing?" she asks.

"Surf City?"

We climb a stair to exit the River and walk toward the feature.

"What's your major going to be?"

"Business, I guess." I point across the way to where Pamela and Ben are searching the Lazy River for, presumably, us.

"What do you think? Friends for life?"

"Nah. They're tennis players. Love means nothing to them." I laugh at her quick-witted joke. "Business, *you guess?*" It takes me a second to remember that was what we were talking about.

"It's sort of expected, right?" I shake my head vigorously to expel some more water. "What's your plan after dance?" Dancers, especially female ballet dancers, have a shelf life and the smart ones know that. I think she's one of the smart ones.

She wants to be s sports physiatrist – a type of physical therapist some of whom work with dancers – but she's hoping to eke out a half-decade from dance first. I admire people who know what they want to be when they grow up. I'm pretty sure going into business is not what I want to do with my life.

"You've got curly hair." Her comment cuts through the sudden wave of depression that washes over me.

"Only when I can't straighten it." I cut it really short before Europe because the guides all said hair dryers are hard to come by. It's grown out enough now that I need to get a trim so it'll lay the way it's supposed to.

"Why? It's attractive." Yeah, I don't think so. My stomach growls. I ate breakfast late – still trying to get on this time zone – but I'm hungry already.

"So we know what my most spontaneous act is – it played on TMZ. What about you?"

"I chased down the ice cream truck last week."

"Really?"

"Yeah. I was hungry, it was hot and I just couldn't stop myself."

"I thought dancers didn't do fat."

"Shhh. We're not supposed to. Don't tell. That way it never happened."

We're laughing as Ben comes running over to us.

"We should go to lunch." He tries to push us into the crowd, but I lift my eyebrows. It's already too late. Alyse and Trevor Grey emerge from the crowd, still in their street clothes, looking around like they're searching for us.

"Crap. What are they doing here?"

"Trevor texted me that she insisted."

"Uh-huh?" Alyse can't drive yet, so she wouldn't be here without Trevor's help. They had a half-day of dance just like Cheyenne and I got a promise from Vic to not bring her anywhere near Calverton.

"I didn't tell her about it." I want to make that perfectly clear as Pamela joins us.

"I mentioned it to Trevor." Cheyenne looks sheepish. I remember what she said earlier.

"His text says he didn't know it was a secret when he mentioned it to Alyse." Ben sighs. His phone is in an otter box so he can take it on water slides. I should probably have that, but I don't. I wonder if Trevor hit my cell phone before he tried Ben, who now shrugs. "No use for it now."

Alyse and Trevor finally reach us through the crowd.

"We've been looking all over for you." Alyse makes it sound like she was supposed to meet us, but of course, that's not true. I don't want her here horning in on my date. My skin crawls at the brief memory of her lips on mine.

"Why are you here?" I pin her with a gaze that I hope is sufficiently angry without freaking out the rest of the group. Alyse hates water slides. She's only here to interfere with my dating life and we both know it. My good time evaporates like morning dew when she sucks me into her nonsense.

"I thought it would be fun. Something cool to do on a hot afternoon."

I open my mouth to say they should leave when Ben tugs on my elbow, which is sore from getting banged on one of the water slides.

"Let it go." He glances significantly at his phone and then at Trevor, who hasn't got a subtle bone in his body.

"I need to take a leak." I appreciate Trevor's attempt. "You can change into your suit, Alyse. The Lazy River sounds *so* relaxing." He winks at me as she passes him. Trevor's our age and just got accepted to a dance studio out of state. I don't like the idea that he's treating my little sister the same way I plan to treat Cheyenne. After casting him a dirty look, I lock eyes with Alyse.

"I didn't invite you. Don't horn in." I keep my voice low. I barely know Pamela and I don't want Cheyenne to feel uncomfortable. I think I might be past caring if I embarrass Alyse, but I don't want to embarrass my friends.

"It's a public place, Peter." Alyse doesn't keep her voice low. "We're just saying 'hi'."

She thus makes me look like the bad guy. Meanwhile, Trevor looks uncomfortable. Maybe he's on the up and up and it was all an understandable mistake. Maybe I would have welcomed him if he'd brought Macaria.

Ben jerks his head in the general direction of the cabanas. I defer to his better sense of people. I wonder what Lucy said to Alyse. Enough that she's mad at me, but I'm irritated enough with her to not care. To make my point, I hold hands with Cheyenne all the way to the cabanas, which I think probably looks possessive, but I'm hoping sends a message.

Fearing Trevor and Alyse have joined our group, my jaws tighten and I get aggressive with my locker.

"When I mentioned it to her, I figured she knew," Trevor explains. "And she acted like she did, then asked me if I'd like to go as her plus-1."

"Where's Macaria?"

"We're not an exclusive thing, man."

"You know Alyse is almost four years younger than you, right?"

"And that's a problem for going down water slides?"

"Pete, back off," Ben orders. "Trevor, treat her like she's 15, got it?"

"Of course. I *love* water slides, otherwise I wouldn't be with –." I bristle and he senses that. "No, um, I'm not saying that right. I wouldn't be here today as her guest. She's too young for me. And, I'll do my best to keep her out of your hair."

Okay, so I could get behind that if it weren't Trevor – hanging out with my little sister. Trevor's reputation involves a lot of drugs and bedsheets. My stomach knots at the thought.

"Fine." Ben seems relaxed. "We're going to Johnny Rockets. You need to take her anywhere else."

Trevor's black eyebrows shoot up into his white-frosted hair.

"I can do that. Hey, can I share your locker? I forgot quarters."

I'm fine with that and he transfers his bag to my locker. Ben wanders toward the showers, leaving me with Trevor who stores his gear while I don a t-shirt. I spent the last two hours laughing with Cheyenne and now my neck muscles are tight and I'm literally grinding my teeth.

"Hey, you want some?" Trevor holds out a 16-ounce Coke. This is *Trevor* so I know it's not just soda. Because of the setting, I almost say "no". There are little kids around and I can get a Coke at Johnny Rockets. I can feel flop sweat sprouting on my forehead and anxiety drying my mouth. The rum tastes bitter mixed with the sickeningly sweet Coke, but I welcome the warmth spreading through my chest and my shoulders immediately relax. I remember on the second swallow that I'm hanging out with Ben and trying not to embarrass myself with Cheyenne, so I hand the bottle back to Trevor, he takes a conservative pull off the bottle before capping it and putting it back in his bag in the locker. I pop a breath mint.

"I promise I'll remember how young she is – give her a good time without – you know."

The soothing warmth relaxes me so much I can't exactly remember why Trevor spending an afternoon with my sister worries me. Ben comes back just as my mind kicks into gear.

"Look, she's only 15 – barely. And you're 18 – what – since February?" Trevor nods. "You're too old for her. Just remember that."

"And we will both hurt you if you don't," Ben warns as he emerges from toweling off his hair.

"I get it. Like I said, I really *love* water slides. Give me a few minutes to get her away."

"And, Trevor - whatever you and Pete just shared – don't drive drunk with her, right?"

Trevor giggles and disappears out the door. I swear, sometimes he acts so gay. I cut a glance at Ben to see how mad he might be. He's toweling off, ignoring me. I pop another breath mint. He smirks and shakes his head. My phone chimes.

CHEYENNE - How do we ditch her?

"Tell her we're going to Riptide Racer." Ben knows Alyse. She hates water slides. She's only here to cause trouble for me. "I'll text Trevor and tell him to take her to Surf City."

We text. I go to the bathroom and wash my face. I didn't shower because curly hair really can't take shampooing more than once a day. It feels good to get the chlorine off my face. My phone dings as I come back to Ben.

CHEYENNE - We're supposed to meet them at the Lazy River in 20. Trevor says he'll take the heat.

PETER - *Is it safe to come out?*

CHEYENNE - He insisted on a go at Bombs Away before and they just walked away.

"Alyse is so going to kill him." Ben chortles. Nobody is better at tapdancing around irate females than Trevor Grey and we'd both pay money to watch his show.

We hastily lock our lockers and join the girls outside. It's warm and humid in the sun. There's the cry of a thousand voices as people plunge stories down thin layers of water. It's hard to concentrate on what Cheyenne says. It's a joke about guys being slow in the bathroom, but I can't tease it out. Rum's not my drink and the sugar in the Coke rushes the alcohol to my head much faster than bourbon and water does. Sweat sprouts on my forehead and trickles between my shoulder blades. Everybody around me moves too fast and passes too close and I lean against a pillar and try not to pass out.

"You okay?" Cheyenne asks. Ben and Pamela turn back.

"Head rush," I murmur. "Sun's hot. Just give me a second."

Ben squats down to look in my face.

"Hey, Pam, why don't you guys go grab us a table and we'll meet you there."

"Sure," Pam says. My head's starting to clear, and Ben's lips tighten into a straight line.

"What the hell, man?" he murmurs. "You can't even have fun at the water park without drinking now?"

"It was a sip. Trevor's idea of a peace offering."

"You're really starting to worry me." Ben sighs. "Seriously. If you can't have fun at the water park without drinking, you got a problem."

"I was having fun until Alyse showed up."

"That's your excuse?" He shakes his head. "At least you didn't talk him into letting you have all of it."

Guaranteed, Trevor needs it more than I do and wouldn't give up his supply. It never occurred to me to ask. Ben knows about my uncle Matt, but I'm not him. I'm not. The momentary floaty feeling eases, and I straighten from the pillar.

"You okay?"

"Better." There's a water fountain maybe 10 yards ahead and I try not to faint before I get there. The water feels good and my body temperature drops. My stomach growls, but I've never been less hungry in my life. As soon as I stop slurping water, my mouth grows dry, so I slurp a bit more before straightening.

"The park's going to wonder about the increase in their water bill." I think Ben is joking and I'm grateful, but now a crease of worry develops between his eyes. "You dehydrated?"

"I don't know. Can you get dehydrated at a water park?"

Ben walks beside me as we head to Johnny Rockets. Inside Pamela and Cheyenne have their heads together in a fast girl friendship. Ben catches my arm before we go in.

"You really are scaring me."

"I'm sorry. Booze doesn't usually go to my head like that."

"Yeah? Do you ever wonder why that is, Pete?"

Ben doesn't wait for an answer. He slides into the booth next to Pamela and I do the same with Cheyenne.

"You okay?" Pam asks.

"Yeah, the heat just got me. I'm good now."

121

I'm not, though. I reluctantly order a burger, eat about three fries and two bites and am glad I opted for water because the thought of Ben's shake makes me nauseous.

"Maybe it's jetlag." Cheyenne barely knows me, but she offers a perfect answer for what's wrong with me. It is still about 4 am for me, way too early for water slides and hamburgers.

After we eat, Ben suggests we do Riptide Racer. My stomach turns ominously. Cheyenne glances at me.

"Lazy River?" she suggests.

"Yeah. Maybe after I've cooled down a little, I'll feel better and we can join you guys."

In the end, Ben and Pamela decide to join us. He texts Trevor.

"Maybe he can direct her somewhere else so we can avoid her."

"You're being kind of mean to your sister," Cheyenne remarks.

"We didn't invite her." She isn't buying my first explanation. "She's tagged after Ben and me most of our lives and sometimes, we just need to ditch her for grownup fun." Cheyenne smiles at me, but her hazel eyes are still skeptical.

"Hey, Cheyenne, let's use the restroom before we head out," Pamela suggests. Ben and I stand up to let them out and then sit back down.

"You're really going to waste that food?" Ben looks like he thinks that's a sin. Maybe it is. What do I know? Gluttony is. Is wasting food? I'd have to ask Helen. "You just drifted off."

"Oh – yeah. Sorry. Just not hungry."

122

"You lost weight in Europe. You sure you're not sick?"

"How do you know I lost weight?"

"Your hip bones. Seriously. I'd have eaten my way through the continent, just to taste it all."

"That was my plan, but their food is too rich – lots of butter and cream. Not as sweet as ours, but heavier."

I ate pretty well in Italy and Monaco – Austria too – but after I met up with Collin in Munich, I was usually too hungover for breakfast – at least until I had a couple of mimosas and then I'd grab a protein bar for lunch because we were running around looking at sights or on a train headed to the next city. I'd never been prone to motion sickness, but the train bothered me. Then dinner – okay, Collin usually dragged me out on the town, and we'd eat the national equivalent of pub food. I know I missed a lot of meals during the last month.

"I hear England has horrible food."

"Maybe not the best person to ask because, by the time I got to England, my stomach was upset the whole time."

Ben frowns at me.

"You maybe should see a doctor, Pete. Something's wrong. I mean, don't you have to be careful about the water you drink in foreign countries?"

"Not in Europe."

"Pete – I'm just saying – it's not like you to not eat."

I agree I'll ask Tilly to make an appointment, and then the girls come back and we head to the Lazy River, even though Ben hasn't heard back from Trevor.

Complications of Dating a Star

Cheyenne

Pete's an attentive date when he's not on the verge of passing out. Great kisser. Not grabby. Knows how to give a compliment without sounding like a creeper. He's got a good sense of humor. He's not gay. The rumors to that effect before he went to boarding school don't fit the guy I'm getting to know. Now he's considered sexy. Tansy swears he's a great lover. That he's playing coy is kind of entertaining. He's different from most of the boys I've dated. I kind of like it. There's a give and take with him that is fun.

Trevor never did text Ben back, but we're committed to the Lazy River since Pete needs to cool down. I don't know what's making him shaky, but I doubt it's the heat. He's pale and his skin feels cool to the touch, not flushed and hot. As soon as we enter the River, he squats down to thoroughly soak himself. I marshal the two-man floaty until he reemerges and settles into the other half.

"Wow, that feels better." Maybe it is just the heat then, though I'm worried because his thigh appears covered with gooseflesh.

"You probably prefer if I don't spin you around in circles just yet."

"Yeah, I still feel a little – better, though. I'm still having trouble waking up in the morning and there was a whole chunk of last night where I couldn't sleep."

"I read a sci-fi novel once where this guy was caught between two universes – or dimensions, maybe – and he sometimes would be in one or the other and then he'd sometimes be in between."

"That sounds like a *Star Trek* episode."

"Is that what it's like?"

"Kind of, yeah. I'll have an hour or two when I feel just fine, and then suddenly I'm not able to keep my eyes open."

"I suspect traveling in a dancers' roadshow is like that too. If this is Rome, it must be Tuesday."

"Literally, I had some days where I didn't know what city I was in."

We're entering the rapids section where one of the flumes enters the Lazy River and Peter hoots and smiles through it, so his vertigo must be easing. He looks over his shoulder as another innertube bumps into us. Alyse looks bedraggled. She's gotten wet and she doesn't look happy about it.

"Maybe we could change partners."

"Maybe we couldn't." Peter's cool, except she kicks his arm. He's out of our innertube in a second, one hand wrapped around her bicep, the other holding down the edge of their innertube so he can lift her free. Trevor and I stare at them as Peter backs her up against one of the side walls and bends his head to speak furiously to her. I can't hear what they're saying because of the sound of the flume behind us, but Peter's face is white and Alyse looks like she's crying.

I've seen this before between my brother Chas and his ex-girlfriend when she couldn't get the message they were over. When they break apart, I glance at Alyse's upper arm, but he didn't leave a mark. Maybe looking angry doesn't translate into physical aggression.

"You two need to get away from me now. Seriously, go away!" Peter holds our innertube to give Trevor a chance to get away from us. "Sorry about that."

"It's fine. Siblings, right?"

Trevor's being too loud, and I know from our years of dance that's a sure sign that he's had something to drink. Ben and Pete don't appear to have joined him in his early afternoon revelry. That doesn't surprise me about Ben. He isn't as squeaky clean as in middle school, but he's a low-key partier, often the designated driver by choice. Pete has a reputation for needing the designated driver, though I've never seen him drunk. He's not acting like Trevor at least, who takes off down the Lazy River pushing a laughing Alyse in an inner tube. That girl's a good actress, no argument.

Pete looks annoyed as he watches them go around the bend. Make up your mind, kid. Either you don't want them anywhere near us or you want to keep an eye on your little sister. You can't have it both ways! Or do you think you can?

I've got two brothers – one older and one younger. Neither of them ever looks at me like Pete looks at Alyse. I can't describe it. Dread and something else mixed. What is that something else? Like boys used to look at me in middle school. Most dancers are slim like willows and I used to be until I suddenly spouted breasts without hips and then the boys *noticed*. And that's kind of the look I see in Pete's eyes. Except for his attraction to me, less than an hour ago was clear. I'm letting Pam too far into my head.

"They're a couple," she said in the bathroom at Johnnie Rockets. *"Maybe he's not as into it as she is, but you watch – he'll let her pull him away the first chance she gets."*

No way! I don't believe he would – except he's acting kind of jealous right now and when he kisses me ... is he picking times when he knows she can see?

"Look at me." I know I sound demanding. He tears his gaze off Trevor's antics – doing a pushup on the innertube over Alyse – and tries to focus on me. His eyes start to wander back. "I thought you were okay with Trevor entertaining her so we could continue our date."

"I am." His answer comes too quickly and he knows it. "It's just – she's so young compared to him."

"You don't think she's all innocent, do you?"

"What's that supposed to mean?" He frowns like he's her father rather than her brother. Maybe if my dad was never around, Chas would act more like Pete is now, but he never even seems to notice when I'm dating a guy. I could probably spontaneously combust in the Lazy River and

Chas would learn about it later, even if he was on an innertube within sight of the light show.

"Just that if they kiss today, it won't be her first time. Seriously – you don't have to worry about her. She's more than capable of handling Trevor."

"I'm also a little worried that he's going to drive with her."

Okay, he has a point, but it's been maybe two years since I've seen Trevor without a little bit on board. He even drank when we danced *The Troll King* together. It seemed to make his performance better if you can believe that. That night I turned the wrong way was the first time I'd smelled it on him, but his performance was flawless, bold, assured, and creative. Yeah, he sometimes got obnoxious when he sought a good time. I guess Pete's right to be worried.

"We'll be here another couple of hours, right? It'll wear off."

Pete's mouth twists. I splash him, hoping it'll distract him. He looks annoyed for a split second and then splashes me back. I try to aim us for a fountain, but I'm not as good at it as he is and I end up going under instead of him. He laughs and takes me under the next one. We battle back and forth for control of our two-man craft until we finally both get drenched. I roll onto my side and plant my lips on his mouth. He tastes of chlorine, cola and – yeah, that's rum. I pull back for a moment and look into his eyes. He's not drunk. He's laughing and he catches the back of my head with one of his long-fingered hands and draws me into another kiss. If this is an attempt to get Alyse's goat, he's making it seem like it's all about me. I go with it and quickly forget my concerns. Alyse who? He has a sister?

When we get back to the loading area, he rolls off the innertube.

"Sorry. I need to go to the locker room for something. I'm feeling better anyway. You want to try Bootleggers Run?"

I laugh and agree. He lifts me out of the innertube, and we climb out. He holds hands with me as we head toward the cabanas. This is a great first date … right up until *they* descend on us. No, not Trevor and Alyse. I forgot Pete is a public figure.

"It's him!" The chick wears a tacky floral swimsuit that is two sizes too small for her pudgy and completely white body. The two girls who are with her are no better. One better not breathe too deeply or she'll spill out the top of her purple suit like a bowl of overripe fruit. The other – well, let's just say she shops at Walmart and leave it at that. "Peter Wyngate!"

Pete's not happy about it, but when they surround him he doesn't seem to know what to do about it. They start peppering him with questions, which he doesn't answer. His replies are oblique enough they don't know he's not answering. For someone whose father is in the limelight, Pete seems woefully unprepared for the attention he attracts. When they ask for a photo, he completely loses any control over the situation he might have had. Instead of saying something about an important meeting he's in a hurry to get to, he says "uh, yeah, I guess." They're not the type of girls who notice something as subtle as lack of enthusiasm. I raise an eyebrow at him and he blushes so deeply I worry he'll pop a blood vessel in that chiseled cheek.

"I'm on a date," he stammers, but they aren't listening. He dips his knees so he's in the frame and I snap two pictures one right after the other and push the phone toward its owner. Alyse steps between us.

"Does this cheap phone belong to you?" she demands, taking it from me. She's asking the girl I tried to hand it to. Clearly, she knows what's going on and is here to rescue her big brother.

"Uh, yes. Thank you. Oh. My. God. It's the sister, Alice."

"Aleese," one of the other girls corrects. "Can we take your picture too?"

"No. I'm not a public figure even if my father is one. Run along, little children."

She's not actually talking to the girls. She's pushing Pete toward the cabanas and signals me with her eyes. I take his arm, but it's like trying to move a concrete wall.

"You're the governor's daughter. Of course, you belong to the public."

Pete's lips twitch like he's going to say something and maybe he is better at protecting his baby sister than he is at protecting himself, but Trevor comes jogging up.

"There you are, my love." He's gained a blatantly Italian accent. "Come away with me. Your gondola awaits. Wave to your adoring public and be off with you."

I tug on Pete's arm and he lets me lead him away. The girls try to follow Alyse. I remember Trevor lifting me to where I needed to be and I know the girls have been outmanned. It's a rescue worth emulating. I pick up the pace walking toward the cabanas.

"Go pee or whatever. I'm going to reapply some sunscreen and meet you here in a few."

Pete shakes off the confusion the girls cast upon him and gives me a quick kiss on the mouth.

"Thanks. I hate all that grabby you-belong-to-us shit."

"No problem." So this is the ticket? Keep him away from his sister *and* the public? I can do that. "Five minutes?"

"Sounds good. And then we'll do Bootleggers."

I make a sound that I hope seems enthusiastic and head for the ladies while he heads into the men's.

Mission

Peter

I've got a mission and I move quickly to accomplish it. No way am I letting Trevor drive my sister home if he's drunk. If we're here for a couple of hours, that's time for him to sober up, but not if he keeps drinking. Fortunately, we're sharing lockers and I've got the key. I pull the Coke out and head into the sink area to dump it. I crack the lid and the smell of warmish cola and rum drifts up to my nose. I hesitate. I'm not driving so I don't have to worry about drinking. I take a sip. Yeah, it's still bitter rum and super sweet soda and I'm not a fan but, man, the way my shoulders relax is welcome. There's not that much left anyway and the two swallows that finish the bottle are just payment for having to put up with Alyse all afternoon. I throw the bottle away and rinse my mouth with water, then pop a breath mint and palm another for when that one's done. I don't want Cheyenne thinking I'm as big a lush as Trevor.

The line for Bootleggers is not so long as I laugh and chat with my date, describing the Arc de Triomphe. I can't remember having such a good time with a girl in a while. Maybe this should be my first-date venue of choice from now on. Yeah, well, I'll have to find out what's similar in Connecticut.

I don't fear heights and I love hearing Cheyenne scream as we shoot down the flume. In the end, the water sprays in all directions and then we spin toward the take-out point. Cheyenne giggles as she slips off my lap so I can roll off the innertube. I stand.

Whoa! Dizzy! The platform at my feet slants precipitously. I drop to my knees in fear of falling and crawl out of the shallow water as my stomach flip-flops. I can hear Cheyenne asking me a question as Ben and Pamela slide out the end of the flume. I can't sort out what she's saying. My stomach twists again and I crawl further from the water, knowing what's coming.

Best Friend to the Rescue

Ben

Pete's in shock, shivering like it's below freezing and not 80 in the shade. His swim trunks are still damp, but I'm worried enough to not care about my upholstery as he sinks weakly into the backseat. Cheyenne looks concerned. This isn't the first time Pete has thrown up at a girl's feet, but he's usually a lot drunker when it happens.

I need to drop the girls off before I take him home. It just makes sense logistically. He's reclining in the backseat with his feet in Cheyenne's lap. He's already getting tanned, so he doesn't look pale, but he clearly feels sick.

"If you're going to hurl, man, use the bag."

"No, I think I got that out of my system," he murmurs. He looks at Cheyenne. "I'm sorry."

"It was fun – right up until you started puking." She seems sincere. She's smiling. He manages a wan smile.

"I hope whatever this is doesn't get you sick."

Pamela gives me this sidelong look that says a lot in a language I don't understand. Skeptical? Disbelieving? Did she think Pete deliberately made himself sick or what?

"I'll call you," she says when I pull up to her door. "Cheyenne, I could give you a ride home."

Cheyenne glances at Pete, who slides his feet off her.

"Go on. I'm good. Watching me turn green can't be that much fun."

"You're sure?"

He nods. That he doesn't try to move to the front is a testament to how weak he's feeling. I think he dozes off on the drive to his house. I pull right up to the front door and he makes it to the foyer before he has to sit down on the bottom stair and put his head between his knees. He's shivering again and his skin feels cold. Nobody seems to be home. I run up to his room and grab a throw from his loveseat to drop over his shoulders then sit down on the stair next to him and wait for him to gather his strength. My phone buzzes.

> **PAMELA – Maybe he should have eaten lunch instead of drinking it. I know he's your friend, but how do you put up with it?**

Pete cautiously lifts his head from his arms.

"How you feeling?"

"Like I'm floating two inches off the floor and at an angle.

MOM – It might be an ear infection. Or even water in the ear. Those corkscrew rides make Jenine want to hurl too.

Jenine is my aunt, my father's sister. Pete burps loudly. He's still got the plastic garbage bag clutched in one hand. He opens it and waits, then closes it and stands, clinging to the stair rail. We left the door open, so we hear Trevor's Fiat pull up and then Alyse comes in the door.

"Go away. I don't want to talk to you right now." Alyse's shrill voice causes Pete to wince, though Trevor grins at her. "We didn't need to leave just because he got sick."

"You don't even like water slides, Ally." I just feel the need to point that out. Trevor pushes past her and steadies Pete on the stairs.

"I can get him upstairs if you need to talk with her."

I thank him and turn to Alyse.

"Has he been feeling punk since he got home?"

Alyse sighs.

"Yeah, some."

"Has he told Tilly or your dad?"

"Dad's never home. I'm not sure what he tells Tilly?"

I open the Contacts on my phone. Because Tilly is often Pete's only "parent", I have her number just in case. I start to text her. Alyse stalls my hands.

"He's not going to thank you for getting in his business."

"It's already too late because my mother knows. She will tell Tilly."

"Then you should stay out of it. Tilly's not our mother. She's just a woman our dad hired to do the job he doesn't want to do."

She sweeps up the stairs. I sigh and head up the stairs to see Trevor has gotten Pete to bed and is closing the blinds. He's talking as he does it, facing the window, so he doesn't see me at the door.

"Did you drink it?"

"It wasn't enough to do this."

Trevor starts to turn and I step back so I'm not in his line of sight.

"Maybe you need to see a doctor and tell him the truth. What happened last spring – that was bad and – I mean, from our perspective, you haven't recovered."

Trevor swings the door fully open to stare at me, then shrugs.

"I gotta head home. Ben's here to lecture you now." He gives me this weird grin as he steps around me.

"How you feeling?"

"Horizontal seems to help."

"Well, call me when you're feeling better – or if you need me to stay."

"I'm going to sleep."

"You need to tell Tilly and – look if you polished off Trevor's bottle – you're scaring me."

"I dumped it. I didn't want him driving drunk with Alyse."

I want to believe him, but it's getting harder and harder and I know that I need to say some things to him before he goes to Yale and I go to Dartmouth. He's like a brother to me and I can't let him go without at least saying what needs to be said. If only I weren't such a coward.

Laurel Ridge

Peter

I wake up feeling like I'm on a life raft a million miles from anywhere. I woke on this cruise ship all across Europe, but the seas are calmer here. My bed, however, is wrecked. I tossed and turned and sweated a ton last night. I haven't had anything to drink since I polished off the bottle the night before the water park – well, except for the gulp of Trevor's magic elixir, so I shouldn't feel hungover, but I kind of do. I mean to strip the bedclothes off my bed, but I'm overcome with a sudden need to hang my head over the toilet. When that passes, I gingerly get in the shower. That helps … a lot. When I come out, it's a good thing I'm wrapped in a robe because the maid is changing out my bed. She's bent over hooking the fitted sheet over the corner of

141

the mattress, giving me a much-appreciated view of her backside. When she straightens, I feel my cheeks flush hot.

"You feeling okay," Karen asks.

"Yeah, why?"

"Your sheets smell like sick."

"I think it's some weird jetlag side effect."

She's older than Tilly, so she has plenty of lines on her face. Now the one between her eyebrows deepens.

"You tell Tilly about it?"

"I haven't. I'll mention it to her."

She nods and returns to making the bed. I retreat to the walk-in closet to find clothes. My cell vibrates. Ben wants to know if I feel up to mountain biking since he has the day off. Maybe if I eat something I won't feel so shaky. I text back that he should pick me up in an hour and set aside my jeans for more activewear. Toast tastes like sawdust, but I wash it and two Tylenol down with coffee and that does settle my stomach.

Alyse and Tilly are both gone somewhere – dance, I guess, so I text Tilly to let her know where I'm going. I raid the fridge for some fruit and make myself a sandwich before Ben gets there. The bike rack on his Jeep provides enough room for both our bikes.

"How'd you get the day off?"

"They're retooling the production line and so they just need the early crew still. I thought I said that yesterday."

I shrug. I don't remember. I still feel a little disconnected from my body, like my head might come loose and float away into the clouds at any moment. I take a long draw off my water bottle. That helps. Ben chose Laurel Ridge, which is a bit more aggressive than I feel up to right now, but since we won't be able to do this again until next summer, I'll tough it out.

Here at midmorning and on a workday, we have the parking lot off Belle Mead Road to ourselves as we unload the bikes and head out on the trail. I hate how Laurel Ridge starts with electrical lines all over the place, but soon we're in the woods and I forget all about it. I love the woods, the way the sun slants through the trees and the scent of pine and mountain laurel. The early part of the Blue Loop is mildly taxing, but as we get deeper into it, I start laboring. Ben stops at the beginning of a black diamond and asks if I'm up for it.

"I sat on my butt on a train too much this summer. I may only be able to do the First even.

"That's fine." He gets his water bottle out while I sit down and try to catch my breath. "It's nice to come here with someone else. I've been doing these all summer by myself."

"I used to come here by myself when you'd be gone to those camps every summer, so maybe we're even."

"I was gone for two weeks, not two months."

"Church camp compared to Europe." Ben makes a face, then laughs. "You know my dad would have paid your way if you didn't have to work?"

"Yeah and I want to go to college, so I said no. You wouldn't have had the same kind of fun if I went."

"No, maybe I would have had more fun."

Ben shrugs.

"You remember the time you went to camp with me?"

"Yeah. That was fun – nerf guns in the dark."

"Is that what you remember?"

143

"What? My walking the aisle? Too little sleep and too much singing."

"You think?"

I nod and fling my apple core out into the woods where I'm sure a squirrel will appreciate it.

"If we stay off the black diamonds, I can maybe do the whole Blue Loop. Not sure. We should go."

The exertion feels good on one hand and exhausting on the other. I drink some water and eat an apple and I feel less like puking. Ben suggests I set the pace until our next break and that makes it moderately easier. There are moments when I feel exhilarated and then moments when I want to bail out. My thighs burn and my hands go numb at intervals. I stop to rest before the Second.

"You're really dragging today. You mention feeling sick to Tilly?"

"I haven't seen Tilly yet. At least I didn't blow it with Cheyenne. She texted me."

"She seemed to be fine with you puking at her feet."

"That was embarrassing."

"Yeah – not your first time, though. How much did you drink – truthfully?"

"I – it was mixed with Coke, so – maybe a shot. Probably less. That's nothing. I wasn't drunk. You saw me."

"Yeah. Maybe you ate something that disagreed with you."

"Maybe. I was pretty sure it was rum, but it might have been scotch. That always upsets my stomach."

"Why?"

I shrug because I don't know. I unwrap my sandwich. Ben sits down to eat his own. A soft breeze dries the sweat on my face and arms. My rib cage feels cold. This is normal.

"What's up with you and Alyse?"

"What do you mean?"

"You just seem more – testy -- with her lately."

"She won't stay out of my business."

"And you're just catching on to that now?"

"This one of those times when you're going to lecture me?"

"Not if you don't want to hear it, but I'd think you'd have noticed the drop off in dates as the year went along."

I noticed, but I don't know the reason.

"It's that untouchable thing?"

Ben just stares at me for a long moment, shrugs as if to himself and takes a long pull off his water bottle, before blowing out his cheeks and saying what's on his mind.

"People suspect you're a couple, Pete. And, half the girls in school were terrified of cutting in on her territory. Your looks, allowance and hot car aside, nobody wants to date a guy who is stuck on his sister."

"I'm not!"

"I know that, Pete, but – did you ever wonder why Pam said no when you asked her out?"

I know Ben. Pamela maybe told him why she wouldn't date me, but he didn't share any of my stuff with her. I trust him.

"Alyse wasn't even in our school then."

"She was around enough that people began to wonder." Ben sighs. "Even I've wondered a few times. Mostly, I know that you wouldn't do that, but – I'm not sure about Alyse. She could have the pick of any guy in school and she's turned them all down."

"Dad doesn't want her dating yet."

"Pete – do you hear yourself? You're justifying it – finding excuses. Her showing up yesterday – she picked the wrong guy to give her a ride because Trevor is on your side, but the fact is – why would she cut in on your date? She hates waterslides. If you and I had been going alone, she wouldn't have cared. That you were there with Cheyenne was what mattered to her."

I sigh. Ben waves at a lone biker who comes by. The scent of the mountain laurel fills my nose.

"What should I do about it?"

"I don't know. Maybe tell her you're not her boyfriend."

"And, if you're wrong, then I look like an ass."

"Yeah, but I don't think I'm wrong. She'll say you're wrong and you will *feel* like an ass, but I've seen that jealous look in her eyes." He pulls his cell out to look at the time. "We have enough time to finish the Second and head to my house. Folks are doing barbecue. You're invited."

I nod, wrap up my trash and drink another swallow of water before Ben straddles his bike.

"You lead, so you set the pace. I'll take over at the next break." I nod because it's been working for me and I push off, my brain full of all the girls who had something else to do this past year.

What Needs Saying

Ben

We stop near the takeoff to another black diamond and Pete's huffing and sweating. I really feel like I should say something about what's worrying me. Pete's weird. Most of the time he takes my direction, but when he doesn't, things can get awkward. Still, someone needs to say something. When he doesn't talk after a few minutes, I sit down beside where he's resting.

"You know I care about you, yeah?"

"Hmm. And you do see things I don't see. And, I think you're probably right. You know I would never – right?"

"Yeah." There's more and he knows when I'm holding back.

"Mostly, right? Why not for sure?"

I sigh. My jaw muscle bunches painfully, and I absent-mindedly rub it. There's no use for it. I need to just say it.

"Pete, you are my best friend and I wouldn't be hanging out with you if you weren't a great guy, but ... the way you drink --." His eyes widen and I plunge forward because I don't want to lose his cooperation before I get the words out. "I don't think you know what you do when you are real and truly drunk. It's scary to watch it."

"I wouldn't have sex with my sister." Yeah, he's getting pissed.

"And the other girls you've had sex with? Do you even remember those?"

He frowns.

"I – I'm pretty sure it didn't happen. Ben, just because girls want their friends to think it did, doesn't mean it happened."

I hope so, but I've been wondering for months and he ought to.

"Or maybe you just don't remember, Pete."

"God, Ben!" We're both remembering Clay Haskell back in our freshmen year when he got drunk and raped Sarah Carmichael. I don't think that's Pete, but if he doesn't remember what he's doing, how can he know?

"I don't want to upset you, but you value me for being honest and – I'm sorry. I just – I don't think you'd have sex with Alyse, but if you don't remember – how do you know?"

He wants to argue. He's never admitted to blacking out and some people don't. I've tested Trevor and the guy's memory gets a little fuzzy, but he remembers what happened. I know Pete's passed out a few times. Passed out

148

or blacked out? He's wondering now too and that's what I want – Right? I lay a hand on his shoulder.

"I'm sorry for freaking you out. I just – I don't want you to hurt yourself."

"I don't drink that much."

"Sometimes that's true and other times you scare me."

I've said enough. He needs time to get his mind around it. I mount my bike to lead the way out of the Blue Loop. He doesn't seem angry with me, but I know that thinking look. There's enough trickiness to the terrain that neither of us can afford to get completely lost in our thoughts. Maybe the exertion keeps him from freaking out before he's processed it.

"Why did you ask me about that camp?" I'm loading my bike on the rack while Pete rinses mud off his calves with his water bottle.

"I always figured you were pretty moral when it came to girls, but I learned some things this summer, and now I'm wondering."

"From Pamela?"

"I talk to more people than Pamela." I want to avoid the truth that Pam sent me looking for answers, but that's not going to help him. "Tansy insists you had sex with her."

"She passed out. I was awake for that."

"And Jillian?" His expression flickers, meaning *he* passed out with her. That's the only answer I'm getting on that. He leans on his forearms to look at me across the roof. I've stressed him out, but he's contemplating things and that's good.

"So, you're wondering if I'm *saved*?" Pete walked that aisle the summer before middle school, the summer his mom left. We came back from camp and he seemed excited and then everything fell apart and sometimes I feel like he sealed a door to that part of his life, and I don't know why.

"I'm wondering about your morality, yeah."

He sits down into my passenger seat and I'm struck that he is still growing taller. I think I've stopped. I adjusted the seat of my car back a notch around Easter and haven't since. I get behind the wheel.

"I guess I don't believe in casual sex." He's staring across the parking lot into the trees. "I want to at least be on the second date and like her. You?"

"I haven't." My cheeks could cook eggs.

"Not even with Pamela?"

"We're going our separate ways in the fall. That's too casual for me."

"That's what I think I'm doing. I swear, Ben. I think they're making it up."

"I hope you're right." I do. I don't want to believe he's that screwed up. "So, let's just go eat some fattening meat. And, talk to Tilly about seeing a doctor, okay?"

He nods. He must know I'm making sense. Maybe he's a little worried about things now. Maybe he'll do the right thing. Sometimes Pete keeps me guessing and – well, I don't know what to do about that. And, maybe, truthfully, it's not really any of my business.

Home-Cooked Meal

Peter

It's rare for me to skip barbecue at the Andersons. Although John's lived in the two-story pretend-colonial all of his life, Helen's folks were military and they lived all over, including Kansas City which has some incredible barbecue. John does the actual grillwork, but she does something with the meat before that makes for a heavenly culinary experience.

My dad doesn't barbecue, though Tilly does on occasion. She's a good cook, but Helen is amazing. Ben, Wes and I help out by carrying bowls out to the picnic table. The weather is perfect for eating out. John calls me over and asks me to hold a platter while he takes corn on the cob off the grill. The smell of the roasting meat makes my mouth water.

"Haven't really had time to talk with you since you got back from your trip." I grin at him and realize I'm looking down on him slightly. When did that happen? "How are you doing?"

"Great."

"Ben mentioned you weren't feeling well."

"It's jetlag. I'm not sick or anything."

John puts a foil-wrapped package on the platter.

"Jetlag can throw some people. Helen and I went on a missionary trip to Africa a few years ago. She hardly seemed to notice the time difference, but it took me a week to adjust to Tanzania. She was off doing physical labor while I was napping." I laugh with him. There are now three cobs-in-foil-jackets on my platter. "When we came back, though, I didn't have any trouble. Well, the first night. I was really tired and then I woke up the next day feeling good."

He's going somewhere and my stomach clenches. But he puts the rest of the cobs on the platter and tells me to go put them on the picnic table. It seems the topic has rested. We sit down and start to eat. After the day's outing, I'm starving, feeling that strange mixture of exhilarated and exhausted that outdoor physical activity provides.

Helen asks me about my trip. Where do I start? Spain was my first stop. Dad signed me up for a Southern European tour, something Yale-affiliated. That was the first week and then I headed to Monaco. Because of the proximity to the French Riviera, a week there made sense, but I'm pretty sure Dad thought I'd be safer with a stodgy young banker than with his hot younger sister. Francesca didn't waste a moment of my time and I got to see her topless. I'd think women would be worried about skin cancer, but I guess not. The male nude beaches – yeah, I do care about skin cancer and even though I don't burn, I kind of think *that* part of my anatomy might.

Helen snorts and shoots a glance at Wes, but I'm pretty sure my comment sailed right over his head. Ben and I were way innocent at that age. Dumb as posts on that topic and still pretty sure girls would give us cooties. I don't think Wes is any more sophisticated.

I still don't know why Alan didn't arrange a chaperone for me in Italy. I only had four nights and three days in Rome, two nights and a day in Venice and then it was onto central Europe. I enjoyed Italy a lot. I discovered a love of architecture. I could have spent my entire two months there, but that wasn't Dad's plan. Of course, I don't say this to the Andersons because they wouldn't understand how Alan's fatherliness smothers me.

I did Austria and Switzerland by myself and wished I had more time. The mountains amazed. I could have hiked for weeks. I met up with Collin in Munich and I realize as I'm telling my story and they're asking me questions that the whole flavor of the trip changed. It became all about the nightlife. Francesca never said no to wine, but she made me get up and go places during the day. I was self-motivated all across southern and central Europe until I got to Munich and then … it's one long confusing memory of drunken nights and hungover mornings.

"You didn't get to Greece," Helen notes.

"Well, I went that time when I was, uh, 11. I'm going back. Visit Greece, Eastern Europe, see more of Switzerland, go to Scandinavia, Wales and Ireland. But when I do it in the future, I'm going to take my time. It was just too much traveling and not enough visiting."

"It's great that you have the opportunity to do that." John's aiming that at Ben more than me. Ben went to Greece as my guest because the folks were concerned I'd get bored – or maybe Mom was worried I'd discover her having sex with some random stranger if I didn't have a playmate. Neither of us truly embraced the experience. I can barely remember much beyond seeing dolphins from my grandfather's yacht in the Aegean Sea.

I want to offer Ben the opportunity to go with me the next time, but he is so prickly about finances as if my father really cares or would even notice the cost of an extra traveler. I'm going to have to figure out some way to convince him, but not in front of his parents.

I'm starting to feel the day's activities so after we clean up, I ask Ben to drive me home. It's still pretty early, but I'm tired and the heavy food is making me sluggish. I thank him at the bottom of the drive and head toward the house. Delivering my bike to the garage, I stare at Dad's Lexus. We weren't expecting him and I don't want to see him. It's never good when he's here and I wrack my brain as to what I might have done to cause him to come home. Nothing. Other than ditching Alyse at Splish Splash, which he shouldn't care about. He's always telling her – used to tell her when he was home – that she shouldn't tag after Ben and I like a lost puppy. No, he wouldn't care about that. So what else might I have done to bring him home? Did he get the European card charges and notice how high the bar bills were? Again, would he care?

Vic is hosting Dad's security guard/driver Marty
upstairs in his apartment, so I can't go up there to distract
myself. Turning off the security-light switch in the kitchen, I
wander into the backyard to just relax on a lounge chair.
Mom's stupid roses are blooming. What's the point of
flowers that don't have a fragrance? I'd take a machete to
them if I had one. I bet nobody would notice.

I open Google on my phone and read the cached pages
for Matthew Dellinis. He'd been something of a playboy
who didn't need to succeed at anything, but he'd owned
some cool resort properties. According to the article, he
died of cirrhosis of the liver while waiting for a liver
transplant. Supposedly, he'd been sober for several years.
Now I don't know what to think. I don't really want to
think.

The light is on in Tilly's suite of rooms off the kitchen
and my curiosity piques when I see a shadow float across
the drapes. She's dancing with someone? Or maybe she's
dancing alone and it's just a distorted shadow. Who would
be visiting her? I'm tempted to go put an ear to her door,
but with Dad home, there are risks to that. Getting her fired
would not serve my purposes. Besides, the heavy meal at
the Andersons has made me tired. I stretch out to look at
the stars. We have no near neighbors, so there's no light
pollution. I stare out toward the ocean, watching the stars as
they twinkle.

I pull myself out of a doze. There's a little bit of
moisture to the air, perhaps the promise of rain, when I let
myself in the front door. The house lays quiet around me.
No, not complete silence. I hear music from the rear of the
house – probably Tilly's rooms. It's a relaxed jazz tune – I

think I did a number to it back in jazz class. I soft-shoe a chain step across the foyer and then head up the stairs. At the top, I could go right to my room or left to Dad's, but I don't want to talk to the parent, so I turn right. Alyse is waiting in my room.

"What the hell?" My heart thumps when I turn on the light and she's just there, sitting on the love seat.

"Where have you been all day?"

"Ben." That's all I'm saying. She can see my clothes and ought to figure out what they mean. There's mud on my hiking boots. If she can't figure it out, she doesn't know me at all. "What do you want?"

"I don't like it when we fight."

"I don't either, so maybe you should stop horning in on my dates."

She turns her gaze away. I've hit a tender spot.

"She's a bitch."

"And you're a cat."

"Don't be like that."

"Like what? An older brother who sees you're alienating people and thinks you shouldn't?"

She frowns. I leave the door ajar and sit down on my desk chair.

"You didn't use to be so mean."

"You weren't interfering with my dates until now. Look, I need a shower before I hit the sack. You should go now."

"You know Dad's here?"

"I saw the car. When did he get here? And on a workday."

"I don't know. I heard his voice when I was in the kitchen."

"Pretending to cook?"

"No, he was in Tilly's rooms. I was looking for you."

The hair on the back of my neck stands up. I don't know what is causing my unease, but it's palpable and I don't want to deal with it while she's in the room.

"I need that shower. I'm sure we'll hear all about it at breakfast tomorrow."

"You don't care?"

"Care about what?"

"That he's screwing Tilly."

I shrug. I'm not sure I believe it and – well, that's a good thing. He won't fire her if he's in love with her. There would be worst stepmothers, I think, especially one who lives on Long Island instead of in Albany.

"Shower. Go. Now."

"Break up with Cheyenne."

"No. Alyse – I'm not your boyfriend and I'm not going to pretend I am."

Her blue eyes widen. Did I score a point? I don't know. She stands up from the love seat.

"I want what's best for you, Peter," she tells me.

"Uh-huh." If my grunt is non-committal, it's because I'm not sure about that anymore. She tries to touch my face and I block her reach. She frowns, but she goes. I lock the door behind her.

Is my dad screwing the housekeeper? I remember the shadow floating across the curtains. Could be, but I can't see it as a bad thing. I turn for the shower because thinking about my crazy family could unhinge me. After Laren, did I care about Alan having some fun? Not so long as he didn't fire Tilly. And, he wouldn't if theirs was more than a professional relationship. Right?

What Happened Thursday Night

Peter

"I need you to drive Alyse to dance today." Tilly wears a normal outfit because it's a day off. Dad does give those to her, though sometimes she doesn't take them to herself. When she does, she often takes Mondays. It's weird to see her in a floral dress with her hair curled, but I like it. She's got a nice figure and she's wearing my perfume. She pours herself a cup of coffee while I sip mine. I'm hungry for my bagel and fruit today, my metabolism revved up by a second day of mountain biking. Ben picked me up in the afternoon and we did BJ's Way at Mountain Laurel.

I'm feeling better, but Ben reminded me of my promise yesterday. He thinks maybe it's not a virus and I should have it checked. Uncle Matthew's death comes to mind every time I think about all the drinking in Europe, but that's ridiculous. I'm 17. People don't get cirrhosis at 17.

"She and I aren't exactly speaking." I've got a date this morning and I'm not letting Alyse ruin it for me.

"You don't have to talk to her. You simply need to drive."

"Where's Vic?"

"Flu."

She acts like Dad wasn't here on Thursday and that's freaking me out. Are they lovers? There's no other way to explain it, right? He bugged out of here before breakfast on Friday morning, so I couldn't ask him and she's acting as if there's nothing to wonder about. And, I'm not shocked really. I mean, my bar for shock is walking in on Mom and Sam. I wouldn't even know about Dad and Tilly if Alyse hadn't told me. They can have sex with each other if they want. Neither is married to someone else. Dad's just 40. Tilly's maybe in her early 30s. So why are they pretending it didn't happen.

"Okay. I'll drop her off and pick her up in the afternoon, but I have stuff to do today."

"She's old enough to be on her own at dance. Are you feeling better?"

Not much gets past Tilly. Karen probably told her about the bed sweating.

"Yeah. I think I'm back on this time zone." I pop an orange section in my mouth. "Helen Anderson thinks I should see a doctor before I go to school."

Helen's never mentioned it, but I don't want to worry Tilly by saying Ben is worried. Ben matters. Helen is just one of my 'moms' who worries about me.

"Something wrong?"

"She's a worry-wart. Thinks I should get my immunizations checked and just have a general physical."

"You were thoroughly immunized before going to Europe, but I'll make you an appointment. There are some vaccines they recommend for college. And, you do seem to have lost weight."

"I grew. Some of my pants are short now." I have lost weight too, but the essence of a good lie is wrapping it in a bit of truth.

She rinses her cup and puts it in the dishwasher.

"Your grandfather called yesterday. Why doesn't he call your cell phone?"

Granddad Mike is old-fashioned. Or maybe he feels calling my cell is too aggressive. He prefers to leave a message for me to call him. I think he might be the only one who still leaves a message on the house phone. I don't know why he doesn't just text me and ask me to call him. I promise her I'll call him.

Alyse comes into the kitchen. She hates eating in here, but she doesn't whine like usual. She's been trying to worm her way back into my good graces for three days now. I usually cave after a few hours. This has got to be a record. Karen is Tilly today, so she slips a plate of fruit and cheese onto the table in front of Alyse.

"Your socks are showing." Alyse's observation annoys me. Why is she telling me something I already know?

"Uh-huh."

"I can help you pick pants after dance."

"Nope." No way in hell are we doing that! I've got other plans for selecting pants. She doesn't need to know what they are. My bagel tastes like butter-encrusted sawdust. Is it possible my sister is also a food witch? I wash it down with coffee. "Eat up. I'm not breaking my word to Mrs. Sims."

She sticks out her tongue. My return gesture is much ruder.

"Peter!" Tilly's eyes are a mixture of humor and anger. "That's just rude."

Alyse gloats while Tilly winks at me from behind her. Butter wouldn't melt in my mouth, though I almost spew my coffee.

"I saw you got an email from Yale." Tilly knows when to change the subject. "Just to remind you to check it."

"Tonight when I get home. I'll call Granddad too."

Alyse makes a face. Lucy must have been harsh with her. I know they talked this weekend. I saw Lucy's car in the driveway. About what? Don't know. Don't care. I take my plate and cup to the dishwasher.

"I'll meet you in the car."

I've been in the driveway, listening to music, for a good five minutes before she comes out with her dance bag. I pull out before she has a chance to buckle up. Our street is quiet enough that I am not likely to have an accident. The Porsche's engine rumbles as I pick up speed.

"Daddy texted me yesterday."

Like I care. I turn onto the Post Road and head toward town. I choose not to ask what the text said.

"You ever planning to talk to me again?"

I could refuse to answer and that might be safest. I'm not as manipulative as she is, so I know there are risks to talking to her. Still, it seems peevish to refuse to speak at all.

"I'm sure eventually I'll thaw, but right now – just be glad I'm giving you a ride."

"Who are you meeting?"

"None of your business."

Tears fill her blue eyes. Crocodile. I resolutely focus my gaze on the road. I'm about 10 miles over the speed limit, so getting distracted is probably a bad idea anyway. I pull up to the curb at Dance Theater instead of turning into the parking lot.

"You're not coming in?"

"Nope."

She hesitates, but she can tell I'm in no mood, so she finally gets out. As soon as she closes the door, I pull out, barely giving a car coming down the street time to stop. I turn the Imagine Dragons song loud and head for the west side of town. The music is so loud and the bass so heavy it is interfering with my heartbeat. I glance down at my speedometer and ease off the gas. No need to get a ticket just because my sister drives me crazy.

Second Date

Peter

Cheyenne's parents live in a McMansion. You know what I mean. It's so new it squeaks and has a patterned and colored asphalt driveway. It's the height of American flash-in-the-pan architecture. That's probably not something to say to the girl you want to hang out with. Except for an immaculately-groomed postage stamp of grass out front, the lot is all house. Her dad owns a string of dry-cleaners, so can probably afford it, but Helen Anderson would point out that the taxes are probably taking away all the house joy. I don't normally have these sorts of thoughts, but for some reason, I'm feeling clear today. Maybe it's that I haven't had a drink since Splish Splash. Four, almost five days. I don't think I've gone so long since boarding school.

Cheyenne bursts from the front door, calling something over her shoulder as she runs to meet my car. I've noticed girls do this with me like they fear me meeting their parents. Which is weird because adults usually like me, at least at first.

"Go before she knows you saw her." She buckles in as if this weren't the first time she's been in my car. I see a woman who must be her mother coming out the front door, but I drop it into 1st and we're off the curb before she can be sure I saw her.

"Why are we running from your mother?"

"She wants to *meet* you. I'm 18 years old. I don't need Mom vetting my dates."

I knew she was older than me. Almost everyone in my class is older than me. If I want a date that is the traditional boy-older/girl-younger, I have to date juniors or younger and that's hard to do after you graduate. I wonder why she doesn't want me to meet her mother. I'll give her the standard BS answers – going to the mall, picnic, sailing. Yada-yada. I turn east on the Mount Sinai Road.

"Where are we headed?" She's rolled down her window and the breeze kisses her cheeks pink.

"Marshall's to start. If I find what I want there, great. If not, we'll go to Walt Whitman."

"You have a whole lot more selection at Walt Whitman."

She's right, of course, but I'm hoping to get in and out before noon and Whitman's is just too overwhelming. I'm committed to the east-running road anyway.

"Can we stop for coffee? I didn't get breakfast."

Sure. I'm a generous date. I can afford to be. I almost never hit the bottom of my allowance and my dad would rather keep me happy. I pull into Strathmore's. I'm not really hungry and I've had enough caffeine, but it's fun to say, "Get what you want." I do like their bagels, but I really can't talk myself into eating again so soon after breakfast. She notices that I order a small Americano and don't get a bagel.

"You still feeling sick?"

"I already ate breakfast, so not hungry."

"I took too long getting ready this morning."

I like that she took her time. She looks good – dark blue yoga pants and a large white cotton shirt over an electric blue camisole. Her hair is caught up in a messy bun. She's wearing tennis shoes, which works with my afternoon plans. I merge into traffic while she eats.

"You don't mind people eating in your car?"

She might have asked that before we got in, but I don't mind. I enjoy cleaning my car and Vic will do it if I ask. With Dad in Albany, he doesn't have enough to do and he's trying to justify his job. With me going to college soon, his driving duties will pick up, I'm sure. Alyse isn't a very good driver even after a professional course. She'll take it again before she stands for her license, but I bet she won't pass. I think Vic's employment is secure until she goes to college. I assure Cheyenne that I'm fine with people eating in my car.

Shopping

Cheyenne

Peter's prediction turns out correct. Marshall's is deserted on a Monday morning and he knows his way around the men's clothing section. Like most guys, he likes his pants too loose on the butt. Although he grabs a few jeans of the ones he prefers, he grabs two of the size I suggest.

"Just jeans, you're not getting dress pants?"

He's looking down at me from his impressive height – he must be 6'1" – and I run a hand up his back, feeling him shiver ever-so-slightly. He lifts a tendril of my hair off my neck, smiling like he really likes the view or my perfume. When we met that first day, he seemed pale, but he's already rocking a tan like he spent all summer in the sun.

"There are much better places than Marshall's to buy dress clothes."

"Are there?" We're flirting and he dips his head to kiss me, gently pushing me back against the wall beside the entrance to the changing rooms. I want to wrap my arms around his neck, but that feels possessive, so I keep one hand on the wall and just lightly touch his rib cage as I feel heat and then something else emanates from him. He steps back from me, holding the jeans he wants to purchase in front of him. Under his tan, there's a warm glow. His full lips curve into a broad smile. I think he might kiss me again, but the dressing room clerk clears her throat behind him and he blushes.

"Let's go meet Trevor at the dock."

"Dock?"

"I want to show you someplace I like."

The taste of him on my lips is delicious as I lick them. His body temperature actually increases.

"Why Trevor?"

"Ben's at work and he's in your dance troupe so he has the day off too. I thought it would be more fun with a few people."

I smile and we go to the cash register to run his card and head back to Port Mallory. He holds doors for me and walks me to the passenger door. The purple Jaguar makes me feel like royalty or a Hollywood star. When we're in the car, he asks me if there's anything I want. I'm content to visit his world and see how much better it can be.

Tough Love

Ben

Work is hard enough after having a four-day weekend, but Alyse is freaking out and blowing up my phone.

> **ALYSE –** Did he tell you he was going on a date with Cheyenne?

> **BEN –** *Kind of.*

> **ALYSE –** What does that mean?

> **BEN –** *He said he was going boating with Trevor and Cheyenne. Suggested I play hooky. It's a beautiful day out, but I couldn't and he knew it. He's just being polite.*

There's a long break, which I assume is because she's in a dance class. My phone buzzes three times while I'm loading the next truck.

> **ALYSE – She's going to hurt him.**

> **ALYSE – He got sick the last time he was with her.**

> **ALYSE – Why aren't you answering me?**

> **BEN –** *I'm working. Pete isn't an idiot, Alyse. And you really should stop hanging on him. You really pissed him off the other day and that might have been one reason he felt sick.*

My thumb hangs over the SEND icon. I hadn't meant to type that, but something resonates. Nothing ruins a date more than puking a girl's feet and, if memory serves, Pete's never had a second date with a girl after that behavior. Was he trying to scare Cheyenne away? Or had the upset with Alyse done it? He was fine before she got there. Of course, he also drank from Trevor's stash, but ….

I backspace over that last bit.

> **BEN –** *I'm working. Pete isn't an idiot, Alyse. And you really should stop hanging on him. You really pissed him off the other day and if he realized girls like him better when you're not around, he's going to decide for you not to be around so much.*

I hit SEND on that one.

My phone buzzes again while I'm working, but Chuck keeps handing me boxes, so I don't look for about an hour.

ALYSE – Don't be silly. He's my brother.

ALYSE – Who have you been talking to? Pamela doesn't like me.

ALYSE – Has Peter said something?

ALYSE – You're mean!

"I'm going to get some water," Chuck tells me.

"Thanks. I need a minute."

I dial Alyse's number. I get her voice mail, so I just say what I would have said had she answered.

"Pete is going to college, Alyse. He's going to be gone for a few months. He'll come back for visits, but you're not going to see him every day. I know that sucks, but it's part of the growing up process. And, you know, he's going to date and someday there'll be a girl who he wants to stick around. You can either fight over him like he's a piece of meat (but you'll lose that fight) or you can accept that your brother will have other women in his life. Don't call me until after four. I'm working. Sorry I have to be the bearer of bad news."

Then I text Pete a short message.

BEN – *Alyse is on the warpath. Might not want to parade your girlfriend in front of her like a sheep to the slaughter.*

That's enough. I need to get back to work. Fortunately, my phone doesn't ring the rest of the shift.

The Boat

Peter

Parking by the port in the summer is always a pain, but I manage to shoehorn my car into a tiny spot.

"Are you worried about your paint job?"

I suspect I'll get just as peeved as Ben would if my paint gets chipped, but I can afford to have it repaired, so I just shrug. Most people are scared to scratch a Porsche, figuring it belongs to a dragon, so I'm not all that worried about it. Trevor's black Fiat is parked a little bit away, so we hurry down the pier toward my dad's yacht. The slip is empty. Maybe that's why he was here on Thursday. He banned me from the yacht unless he's captaining last year, so I hadn't really thought about it. I don't want to think about any of it. Meanwhile, Trevor and Macaria are practically having sex in my boat, which doesn't have a cabin.

175

"Get a room, you two." My quip makes Cheyenne giggle, but Trevor and Macaria have no shame. They slowly disengage from their clinch. Fortunately, Macaria is wearing a swimsuit under her too-short dress, otherwise, small children might need their eyes covered.

"Got to have something to do while we wait." Trevor runs a hand over his frosted hair. "I'd have checked everything if I had keys."

Uh-huh? He's not boat-set. I doubt he'd know a rudder from the ignition. I drop into the blue-and-white Malibu, sliding the cooler into the far corner before turning to offer Cheyenne a hand down. It's not that she needs my help, but that I'm a gentleman. Ben's questioning of my sexual exploits bugs me. I have no memory of being anything but a gentleman with the girls I've not succeeded with.

I run through the safety check, doing the quick math for the gas. I have twice what I need to get to our destination and back. The transponder works. I file a float plan. I don't want a lecture from Captain Russell. Macaria climbs up on the dock while I'm doing the check so she can burn a butt. She's kind of short and willowy with dark curls and denim-blue eyes. I remember she used to dance ballet. I want to be a good host.

"How are you doing, Mac?"

"Good. Working at my dad's hardware store."

"Sounds like fun."

"You're kidding me, right?" She pushes a dark curl behind one ear. "Have you ever been to a hardware store?"

"I have." Ben's dad used to take us around on Saturdays. I remember that you weigh nails. I say that as proof that I've been in a hardware store.

"He's a funny guy, Trev." Her blue eyes twinkle. I never really know if she's serious about anything. I think she's high. Not completely wasted, but like Trevor, she almost always has something on board. I couldn't function like that. I can't even maintain a low simmer with drinking. Half a drink before studying works fine. A whole drink means I don't do my assignments.

I don Paul Bellamy's accent. "I'm a real comedian. Hang around. I'm here all afternoon." I run through the checklist again. "We're ready. You ready?"

She's one of those smokers who takes the smoke deeply into her lungs. I don't get it. It smells awful and it makes everything about you stink. She's pretty, but she already has lines around her eyes and I can kind of imagine what she'll look like when she's Tilly's age. Not attractive. She tosses away her butt and clamors into the boat. I motor us out slow because there's a lot of boat traffic in the harbor even on a Monday. As soon as I clear the breakwater, I want to open it up but Hillary Cavanaugh is slowly sailing his daddy's yacht across my path.

"What the hell, man?" Trevor gestures rudely at Hil who sees him and flips the European f-you sign at him, laughing with the girl on his deck. I don't recognize her, but her hair's done-up in this elaborate crown-like arrangement, totally inappropriate for boating. "Can't you go around?"

"Not without causing a wake."

"Who gives a shit?"

It breaks the rules of boating and I hated it when I owned my sailboat. Of course, mine was a 2-man that barely rode above the waves, so I sat in people's wakes. I wait for the way forward to open, idle forward so as not to cause a ripple, then glance around and open it up as I head to Cormorant Island. You can't talk when we're on step, so Trevor and Macaria climb in the front seats and get back to undressing one another. Cheyenne stands next to me, hand braced on the windscreen. Her messy bun is no more, and she's not freaking out about it. She's smiling. I'm glad she's enjoying herself.

Ingenue

Cheyenne

I've never felt like this before. Peter's attention has to be on piloting the boat, but he glances at me occasionally and I feel like I'm the most important person here. Trevor and Mac are rolling around in the front seat, swapping every bodily fluid short of copulation. They've always been like this. There are stories of Mac getting laid in the dressing room bathroom when we were in junior company. She quit dancing last year or I might not have gotten Rebecca's recommendation to Joffrey. Mac is tough competition. Was.

This boat is the epitome of cool. I imagine myself as a 1920s ingenue headed to a speakeasy out in the Bay. If Peter had warned me, I would have worn a flapper dress. I remember rocking one of those for a jazz number a couple of years ago. You can't help but feel glamorous wearing red sequins with a silk fringe.

I lean into his ear and he steadies me with one hand while he steers with the others.

"You really know how to make a girl feel like royalty."

He grins at me with a "wait to see what's coming" look and I grin back. This is going to be the best few weeks of my life.

Fun on the Island

Peter

When we get to the island, I swing wide to enter my little cove, feeling like I'm letting them in on a major secret. The day feels momentous. I climb out to lift Cheyenne over the water. Trevor makes a show of carrying Macaria to the shore. She clowns around that he's her hero.

"What is this place?" Cheyenne scans the beach, perplexed. It's nothing special as a beach — sand, seagrass and sea rocket. Near a pile of stinking seaweed in the lee of a big rock lays a treasure trove of purple quahog shells so beautiful they were once the currency called wampum. I pick up a reddish bay scallop shell and offer it to Cheyenne. She smiles and slips the shell into her pocket.

"So, really, what is this place?" Mac dons sunglasses, so it's hard to see her eyes. She smiles when Trevor hands her a sea star. When he's not looking, she tosses it back in the ocean. I never pegged Macaria for a closet environmentalist. I always toss the stars back too. It seems cruel to let them die of dehydration.

"There's an abandoned house up there." I point, then indicate the trail. "I enjoy coming here sometime."

"Cool. It's like a Scooby Doo Mystery." Trevor scans around. "Well, if the Scooby gang was actually cool, you know. None of us really fit any of them."

"I think I'd make a great Thelma." Macaria fluffs her dark curls to a Thelma-adjacent style, but she's thin and willowy, not square and chunky, and wearing a vagina-length dress in a bold red geometric.

"That would make me Daphne." Cheyenne taps her chin in an appropriately Daphne-like gesture, then cracks up laughing. "Definitely not."

"That would make me – naw, not Shaggy. Maybe Scooby-Scooby-Roo." Trevor manages to sound pretty much like Scooby. He leaps to the top of the rock with dancer grace, striking a surprisingly Great Dane-like pose.

I swallow my glottis and manage a respectable impersonation of Shaggy.

"Zoinks. We're going to need some Scooby snacks." I pull the insulated picnic basket out of the boat.

That phrase hurts because my voice is a lot deeper than Matthew Lillard's, so I clear my throat before continuing, trying to match Fred's rhythm of speaking.

"It might be a little spooky at night, but I have to pick up Alyse at 5, so we won't be here then, gang."

I drop the cooler in the sand and run at the boat, my foot meeting the bow before I flip over backwards and land with my jazz hands raised to the bright sky. Cheyenne breaks into a riff from *Footloose* and finishes with a hip-hop sequence. Macaria flits across the sand on pointe and then leaps into Trevor's arms. He lifts her skyward, but she's clearly out of shape because she can't hold it long. Cheyenne doesn't embarrass her by showing her how it's done. Maybe she doesn't want to embarrass me. Could I hold her over my head for as long as Trevor held Macaria? We all laugh and Trevor pulls out a fifth of vodka. He takes a pretty good slug and so does Macaria, neither of them wincing at the burn. Cheyenne takes a sip, grimacing. I pass it on to Trevor unsampled.

"Seriously?"

"I can't pilot the boat loaded, right?"

He mugs a face. Is Cheyenne relieved? Maybe a little. I don't know her well enough yet to know. I lead the way through a vanguard of beach plum and then up the bluff to the actual estate.

"Wow, this really is like a movie set – *Laura Bow in The Colonel's Bequest.*" I have no idea what Macaria is talking about. She's taken off her sunglasses to stare narrow-eyed at the greenhouse. "All we need is Spanish moss."

She fishes a cigarette out of her pack and lights it.

"Watch your butts," I warn. "Lots of dry grass. We don't want to cause a fire."

She smirks, but when she's down to the butt, she thoroughly grinds it into the dirt. We press our noses to the windows.

"Who owns this place?" Trevor takes a draw off the vodka.

"I think a bank. My uncle Matthew looked into buying it before he got sick and died. It was in receivership then."

"Why didn't he buy it?"

"I think he meant to, but he got sick." A wave of sadness washes over me like a tide. Trevor bumps my arm and offers me the bottle. I shake my head. Vodka tastes like gasoline to me. I'm surprised Mac can stand it. It must combine with the burned carbon in her mouth and taste like burning gas. He turns to Macaria and says something that must be a line from an old movie. He uses one of those affected WASP voices from those old black and whites. I laugh because he's got great comic timing. Macaria responds in like manner, slipping into the role of a debutante of past decades. Cheyenne helps me spread the blanket and we dole out sandwiches, chips and sodas. Karen threw in some fruit too.

Cheyenne helps me spread the blanket and we dole out sandwiches, chips and sodas. Karen threw in some fruit too. Everything feels perfect. The sun warms the air, but the ocean breeze keeps it comfortable. The old house as backdrop to our picnic makes the perfect setting for four dancers. These are my people and I entertain thoughts of rejoining them.

Mixed Drinks

Peter

The Twenties schtick continues. Cheyenne's not as good at accents as the rest of us, but she's better at body acting, striking poses that make us all laugh. Trevor grabs my soda and I'm about to say he's going to drink my spit when he tips the vodka bottle into the can.

"A little mixed drink's not going to make you drunk."

It won't. I'm no light-weight. I usually drink my booze straight. I sip it. Too much sweet soda. I take a swallow and add some more vodka. Better. My sandwich tastes good and the juicy tangelo offsets the salt of the chips.

"Mr. Grey, make love to me or lose me forever." Macaria sounds remarkably like that chick from *Top Gun*. Laughing, Trevor and she run giggling around the side of the house.

"It's a beautiful spot," Cheyenne remarks. "I can see why you like to come here. How'd you find it? Because your uncle was thinking of buying it?"

"No. Ben and I found it when we were out sailing. We were over at Mt. Calamity and we sailed over here. There was a dock back then. Then a couple of years ago, Matthew was visiting. I took him sailing and brought him here. He was a resort owner – several of them – and he saw the potential."

"You have a sail boat?"

"No. I sold it to Ben a couple of years ago."

"Why?"

"I wanted the speed boat and dry-docking both would have been a pain." I scoot closer to her, gaze dwelling on her pink lips. She pulls her shirts off over her head and then slides her hand up my chest to gently pull me in for a kiss. She tastes of mustard and tomato with just a hint of vodka. I settle her onto her back on the blanket and we might as well be in another old movie. I kiss her throat. She tugs on my shorts and I gently still her fingers. "Not here." Macaria moans from around the house. "I've got nothing to prove to them."

Her hazel eyes look deeply into my eyes.

"Gentleman?"

"Yeah, maybe. I want our first time together to be special – maybe in a bed – at least not within earshot of another couple."

"That's sweet. I appreciate that. You know I'm not a virgin, right?"

"Never thought about it." It's an invitation to explain that I am, but it's not cool in our class to admit that we are, so I don't. I kiss her instead.

Salt prickles on the back of my neck as the sun shines down on us. The effects of the food start to slow me, muddle my head. I roll onto my back to look up at the clouds, which remind me of fluffy cotton balls.

"What do you see?" Cheyenne's pinning my left arm to the blanket. "I see a clipper ship."

I scan the sky and, sure enough, there's a formation that looks like sails shredding in a high wind.

"There's an archer."

"Hmm."

My legs feel like they're melting into the blanket. I yawn. Cheyenne's warm on my arm. I don't know how much time passes, but I wake thirsty. Cheyenne shifts and blood returns to my fingers. I sit up, rubbing the pins and needles out of my arm. There's no sodas left and the bottle of vodka is empty. Trevor brought it, so it was his right to drink it all, but I'm irritated. I take it to the tap and fill it with water, then drink about half the bottle down. I go back to where Cheyenne is trying to untangle her hair and offer her the other half. She's still in her bra. Some chicks are gorgeous in clothes but when you see them without that covering, they're flabby. She has definition in her abs. I don't look too bad until you compare me to Trevor. Dance is the ultimate exercise.

My phone is in the picnic basket.

"We need to go if we're going to get you to the studio in time." I show her the screen. She reaches for her shirts. I head in the direction Macaria and Trevor went. They're asleep and I don't go into the bushes where they're barely hidden. Trevor wakes up as soon as I kick his bare foot. I go back to pack up the picnic. As far as I can tell, I'm the only one who comes out here, but I don't leave anything behind. I would make Macaria collect her butts if I thought she'd do it. Before we head back to the beach, I wash my face at the tap and stop feeling like I'm going to fall asleep on my feet.

We're almost to the breakwater, but still on step when the yacht crosses our path, pushing off from Mt. Calamity. Apparently, Hillary is just sailing back and forth delaying other boats. It feels deliberate. I see Hil on the deck and there's the chick with the perfect hairstyle. She's spent hours getting it that way to go yachting. I don't change course. I nudge the throttle a little forward. Cheyenne's eyes are wide when I glance at her. Trevor glances over his shoulder, his face white. And then I abruptly turn aside, raising a wake that washes up onto the yacht's deck. I glance over my shoulder to see her hairstyle is ruined. Hil is soaked. I swerve around to their stern and continue toward the harbor.

Trevor laughs, Cheyenne frowns, and Macaria scowls. Girls don't make sense. That was funny as hell. I idle down, slowly working my way through the boats in the harbor. Why is Captain Russell waiting at the berth when I get there? My heart thumps. Did I miss a phone call, and something is wrong with Alyse?

Consequences

Cheyenne

Pete idles down the boat as we enter the breakwater. Macaria and I are both frowning, but Trevor's laughing like a hyena. Pete's pleased with himself, I can tell, but he's shooting glances my way as if he's rethinking his position. Someone could have been hurt. I just never expected him to be like that. We float around the larger boats in the harbor and Pete aims for the big slip his speedboat berths in. According to Trevor, there's usually a big-assed yacht there too. A tall, broad giant of a man is leaning against a mooring post, massive arms crossed over his muscular chest.

Peter straightens and expertly brings the boat into the tires that bumper the wharf.

"Hi, Captain," he says.

"Need to talk to you, Pete."

"Um, why?" He knows. His right hand fists behind his back. You'd never know it by how certain his voice is.

"Didn't you think they'd call the harbor master on you?"

Peter pauses. It's not a sigh. It's a gathering of himself. He looks this man right in the eye and says exactly the right thing.

"I'm sorry. I didn't see them until it was too late. At least I didn't hit them."

Captain glares at him, his gaze sweeping all four of us. I can't tell if Peter's telling the truth or not, but Trevor looks this man right in the eye.

"Harbor gets kind of crowded."

"Don't dig a deeper hole," Captain advises. "Pete, I'm letting your father know about this. What the hell were you thinking?"

"It was an accident – well, an accident avoided. Why are you mad at me for avoiding it?" There was no avoidance. It was deliberate. I hope my face doesn't show that. If Peter's decided to lie, I'm not going to work against him.

"Pete, I'm not stupid and neither were the people on the boat. Nothing you say to me is going to keep me from calling your father and you talking right now is likely to make what I say to him even harsher."

Peter's not looking directly into his eyes now. I want to stop this from happening, but I don't know this man so I can't think of what will prevent him calling Peter's father. Governor Wyngate is in Albany. Can the man just call him up like that? I think he's going to call the housekeeper and I get the feeling Peter can work her around.

"Yes, sir." Peter's sucking up and Captain shakes his head.

"Pete, sometimes I really don't know about you." He puts his left hand out to the side. "Good kid. Smart kid." He puts his right hand out to the other side. "Complete foul up." He drops his left hand and just lets the right one linger there. "If you would ever just stop and think before you do things…." He sighs. "Give me your boat keys."

"What?"

"You heard me. Until I hear from your dad, I'm not letting you use the boat. Hand them over or I'll drag it up into drydock."

Peter hands the key over, his mouth tight, but not arguing. Can this man take his personal property from him? Captain scans our little group again.

"You had fun at the expense of someone else. Now, your fun is over."

He walks away. Peter shakes his head.

"He's overstepping," Trevor mutters. "Who does he think he is? He owns a fucking repair shop."

"Really?" Macaria asks, irritated. "What if he'd miscalculated?" She points at Peter, hits me with her laser blues and then sneers at Trevor. "Somebody could have been hurt. Spoiled rotten rich kids. Idiot boys."

She scrambles up onto the pier and strides away. Trevor swings up and chases after her. Peter looks askance at me. Nervous.

"You want to yell at me too?"

He's asking, so I'm honest.

"What you did – that was dangerous. And, pretty rude."

"Hil's a jerk."

"But jerks don't deserve to be drowned and – well, someone could have been hurt."

He nods. Macaria's right. Yeah, it was fun, but bringing it right up to the edge like that – it was risky. I think Peter knows that. His green eyes are downcast.

"I apologize. I wasn't thinking about what you and Macaria would think. I'm sorry. I won't do it again."

I smile and we walk back to his car holding hands. Trevor's Fiat is already gone. I wonder if he caught up with Macaria.

Snooping

Peter

Cheyenne goes into the studio before I do because I say I need to get something from the back before I go in. That's not really true. I got a text from Ben telling me that Alyse is upset and I don't want to get into a fight with her over Cheyenne. Thinking about what I did to Hil, I dawdle for five minutes, which means I enter a few minutes before Alyse's class ends. Her face is flushed with activity when I glance through the window. I see her dance bag in one of the open lockers and I wander over there.

Dad texted her yesterday? Why? Her lock screen code is her birthday. There are no texts from Dad. Deleted? Email? I open her email app and take advantage of her saved password. It's an email train – Alyse complaining about my attitude since I got back from Europe. Dad explaining that I'm probably just jetlagged. Alyse worried that I'm not feeling well and Tilly doesn't care. Dad defending Tilly and me and suggesting jetlag again. Alyse complaining that I ditched her at Splish Splash. Dad asking her if she had a ride home. Alyse asking him why he came home Thursday night and was gone Friday morning. He was picking up the yacht for a meeting and just using the house like a hotel. He spoke with Tilly about Alyse's concerns. He thinks Alyse should stop annoying me deliberately.

I'm keeping my eye on the observation window to assure I won't get caught.

ALYSE – Dad, are you and Tilly having sex with each other?

My breathing quickens. I don't want to know. It doesn't matter. I'll be at school in two weeks. Besides, knowing about my other parent's affair didn't work out well five years ago. And, the class looks like it's over. I shut down the app and put the phone back where I found it, whipping out my own. I'm an experienced snoop. You don't get caught if you look like you're not doing anything unusual.

Alyse doesn't try to hug me this time, just reaches past me to grab her bag. She's so delicate looking in her black leo and pink tights.

"You took the boat out." Observant. My hair is probably tousled, and my cheeks feel a little sun-kissed. My tan should be glorious by tomorrow, a golden brown that most people cannot achieve even with products. DNA is a lovely thing.

"I did. Felt good to just mellow out." I yawn. "Look, little sis – I don't want to fight with you. Can we get past all this?"

She doesn't relent immediately. She sulks better than I do. Longer too. Cheyenne announces the role roster for next week's performance and Alyse breaks from me to check it. She returns euphoric.

"A solo and advanced to the main company."

"That's great." It really is. She's been trying to make the main company all year and this summer intensive was all about that. For the first time since I got back from Europe, I feel happy for her. I give her a sideways hug to show I'm proud of her. She's learning. She doesn't try to make it full frontal.

I'm feeling good as I drive home, until I see Granddad Mike's car in the circular drive. I wasn't expecting him and that worries me.

"Peter, need to talk to you." He's standing in the doorway of Dad's study. He's keeping his voice light, but I know he knows. Alyse frowns. I go into the study – a large room with Dad's desk in one corner, several couches and a full bar against one wall. He closes the door in Alyse's face. "Buzzing boats? Since when are you Collin?"

I did spend a month with my cousin Collin this summer. He's a bully. He thoroughly enjoys being a rich kid and he's never had a friend like Ben to straighten him out. Did he buzz boats? He's never mentioned. I don't want to be anything like Collin.

"I wasn't paying attention and the boat was just there. I won't lie. I don't like Hillary and I kind of liked splashing his girlfriend, but I know I shouldn't have. And, I didn't plan it."

Granddad Mike sits down on the tufted-leather sofa and sips from a highball glass. I don't smell alcohol. It's probably water. Much as I want to go pour myself a stiff one, I know that's a stupid idea. Don't give adults ammunition. I get a glass from the bar and fill it with flavored seltzer.

"Showing off for a girl?"

I sit down on the opposite sofa, a slouchy suede in a russet brown.

"There was a girl, but I didn't plan it that way."

"I know Hillary's father. They're a family of jerks. That doesn't mean you shouldn't be more careful. The harbor's not a place to kick up wakes."

"I wasn't in the harbor. We were out on the bay."

"Jake Russell said you were just outside the breakwater. You should have been slowing down by then."

"I was and then he was just right there in front of me. You don't think I'd deliberately try to hurt someone, do you?"

His eyes narrow.

"Of course not. I was young once too. And, you're in luck. Your father and Tilly are neither of them answering their phones, so Russell called me. I promised I'd take care of it. I won't tell Alan so long as you promise me it won't happen again."

"It won't. It can't. Russell has my keys."

"I'll get them from him. I'll keep them through the weekend."

I open my mouth to protest, but then just sip my seltzer. Grapefruit was not the best choice. There's an underlying taste that I'm not enjoying.

"Sure. I probably deserve that. I did promise Alyse I'd take her out one last time before I go to school."

"You'll still have time. She's got that big dance thing this weekend anyway."

Friday night. That still leaves Saturday and Sunday. It won't do me any good to fight it. I sip more seltzer.

"How are things with your sister?"

"Better." I top off my glass with the bottom of the bottle. "Lucy must have said the right things to her."

Why do I call my grandmother Lucy? Because that's what she calls herself. Her children called her Lucy and her grandchildren call her Lucy. I used to be a little embarrassed explaining that to people who asked, but now I'm starting to see it. She's Lucy – not just a wife, mother or grandmother. And, then I call my mother Laren in my head, though I still call her Mom to her face.

"Did you doubt that she would?"

I laugh. I didn't doubt, but I feared she'd make things worse. I don't want people thinking I'm dating my sister and I'm embarrassed to be physically uncomfortable every time I'm near her, but I still love Alyse. It's been me and her against everything for as far back as I can remember. I don't want that to change. I just want – I want – yeah, I don't know what I want.

"You should maybe talk to her yourself. It's a different perspective than mine and – well, men should listen to women. They see things we don't see."

Maybe Lucy can explain why my sister thinks we should date each other. Or maybe she can explain why every cell of my body is screaming I need a drink right now.

"Where'd you go?" Mike's staring at me as I startle out of thinking about the taste of Four Roses.

"Actually, thinking about how badly I would feel if someone had gotten hurt."

"And?"

"Bad. I didn't mean for it to happen."

"That's good. Next time maybe you'll pause before you do something similar. A part of being young is doing things that won't make sense a few years in the future."

That's good because I'm beginning to think nothing in my life makes sense and I'd hate it if this were the rest of my life.

"You and I need to go fishing next week."

I don't really care for fishing. It's not that I don't like to eat fish – I really love seafood – but I don't like the whole wriggling worm on the end of a hook thing. I empathize with the fish, I guess. But I absolutely love hanging out with Granddad Mike for a couple of hours. We don't talk a lot, but it's the most companionable time I spend with anyone but Ben.

"I got your dad to go with me this summer. Alyse too. Separate times."

"And?"

"She made me bait the hook and then she wanted me to thump the fish for her."

We laugh together.

"And Dad?"

"Pretty much the same." I almost snort seltzer water. Grapefruit bubbles might hurt the sinuses.

"Well, then I have to redeem this branch of the family." I bait my own hook, though I don't like thumping them. "Where and when?"

"We'll do my pond. Monday morning?"

That's an early morning, but I should be sufficiently recovered from Saturday night. I agree to sunrise at the far side of his pond. He stands.

"I should get going. I'll see you Friday night."

We embrace in a heart-felt hug and I walk him to the driveway. I stroll back into the house and pause in the foyer. I consider whether to get that drink now, but I decide to go swimming instead.

Mugged by Mom

Peter

The Yale email asks a bunch of questions that I'm pretty sure I answered before I went to Europe, but I dutifully fill them out again as if I've never seen them before. My cell buzzes as I hit SEND and I glance at the screen. Damn! Mom! Great!

Why do I answer? I always answer. So I answer.

"Hey."

"There you are!" Laren sounds breezy cultural – think yachts and tennis whites. "You haven't called me since you got back."

I didn't. I would have called if I'd decided to board that plane for Miami because I can't rent a car on my own, but there's no reason to call her if I don't need her and I didn't.

"Been kind of busy getting back on stateside time and getting ready to move to Connecticut."

"You must come down before you go."

Uh, no! I'm not doing that. My days are scheduled from now until the day before I go. I don't have time to jet to Miami.

"Dad's got me pretty booked." Yeah, I'm lying. I haven't talked to Dad since that first morning over a week ago. I'm betting she doesn't want to talk to him any more than I do.

"But the boys would love to see their big brother."

I do like my brothers, even though they're little kids. Well – Case is almost five. He maybe was conceived by the time I walked in on Laren and Sam. Counting on my fingers says he was. The divorce decree was barely dry when he was born. Calen is now three and a half. I doubt he even knows who I am since I last saw him at Christmas.

"Maybe I can come down for Halloween." I would enjoy taking them around for candy. I kept doing it with Alyse until she outgrew it and I played bodyguard for Wes and his friends for a couple of years. They still go but they didn't need someone last year and I found I missed it.

"I was hoping we could spend some time together."

My gut tightens. Uh, no! I don't wanna.

"I'm sorry, Mom. I can't."

She huffs. It really does sound like that over the phone.

"I suppose I could come up there."

She could. Planes go both ways, after all, but I'm not really in the mood to deal with her.

"I really do have a lot going on right now and Dad's in Albany, so he won't let you stay here."

Screech! I hear her mind go full-stop, slam on the brakes, fling someone into the windshield. Yeah, she remembers why she's not allowed to stay here when Dad's not around.

"Alyse would love to spend time with you if you come, but I'm scrambling to get everything done before I go." I babble about not preplanning before going to Europe. I give her ample opportunity to ask me about my trip, but nothing is ever about her children. Laren is completely about Laren. "But like I said, Alyse would love a visit."

"I'm not that interested in spending time with her."

Ta-da-dum-da!

"She has a dance performance tonight. You could be here to watch it if you went to the airport right now."

Laren came to every one of my performances, even when she was in Florida and pregnant. She's been to none of Alyse's performances. That's why it's odd that Alyse wants her in her life and I don't particularly. She loves me too much and Alyse far too little.

"I'll see you at Halloween." That works for me. She doesn't indulge her behaviors around Sam. I'll text him once we're off the phone. I don't know what he knows, but he never leaves us alone when I visit.

"I'll call before. Gotta go. Alyse needs a ride to the studio."

I hang up. Alyse doesn't have to go for an hour yet. My neck tightens and my stomach boils. I'm in the closet looking in my stash areas before I even realize what I'm doing, but I've cleaned myself out and haven't missed it until this morning. Sweat sprouts on my forehead and my mouth goes dry. I know what to do about it.

Fine alcohol is often shipped in cheap bottles, so even though I've tossed all mine, I know where the back stock is kept for Dad's bar. I slip into the pantry and ease open the cabinet. The case of Four Roses tantalizes. I grab one bottle, stuffing it into the backpack I grabbed. Wouldn't do for Karen to see me absconding with a full bottle to my room. I turn into the study as I head back upstairs and pour myself two fingers neat. My eyes unfocus for a moment and then my shoulders relax, and my headache goes away. I've just consumed the equivalent of two mixed drinks before breakfast and Dad's not even home. Maybe Ben's right. What is the line between taking the edge off and developing a drinking problem?

I clean up after myself because nobody uses the study when Dad's away. I get back to my room without encountering any stops. I hang the backpack on its hook. I think it'll be fine there. I brush my teeth with a lot of paste, swish with mouthwash and pop a couple of breath mints. Maybe I pushed it a little. I feel like I could run a marathon and come in first. If Dad were here right now, I could tell him I want to be an architect. I think I want to be an architect.

"Hey, Tilly," I say as I enter the kitchen. "How are you this morning?"

She gives me an odd look while I pour coffee.

"I'm good. How are you?"

I choose not to tell her about Mom's call. I offer to drive Alyse to dance.

"Of course, if you want. You're on New York time, finally?"

"Yeah. I feel great."

I can see what Dad might see in her. She's pretty in a no-nonsense way. I sit down with coffee and slowly peel a banana. She says something and I have to work to bring my attention back to her. Did I email Yale?

"Yes. I answered all of their questions. I think I answered them before."

"I think you did too, but maybe they just sounded the same. Dr. Reardon called. He's postponing your appointment until Tuesday. Something about the Hep A vaccine shipment being delayed. It'll be here Monday."

"Why do I need a Hep A vaccine?"

"It's recommended for college along with a meningitis shot."

We're chatting back and forth when Alyse comes into the kitchen.

"Why do we have to eat in here when the dining room is so sunny?"

"It's easier to clean up." Tilly and I laugh because we say the same thing at the same time. "Psych." I make her smile. The room has a warm glow around the edges, kind of like the sun is shining here too. "Grab some breakfast so we're not late."

"We're not going to be doing that much today – just setting up."

"Doesn't mean you can be late. Remember, early is on time, on time is late."

"You're in a cheery mood this morning."

"It's a nice day out."

I glance at my phone and try to calculate how much time we have before we need to be there. It's 8:15 and we're supposed to be there at 9:00 and that's ... whoa, it's not quite calculating. I pour myself another cup of coffee. We've got time and I'm feeling the bourbon now.

Lela Markham

I ask Alyse about the role she's dancing. It's a ballet jazz fusion to an old Frank Sinatra song. I love the idea. Tilly leans back against the counter, smiling at our interaction. I'm almost wishing I'd continued dance training. I can imagine the moves. It would be fun to do them.

"We'd better get going." Alyse looks at her phone. Ten minutes have flown by. I'm on my feet, moving toward the back stairs.

"I'll meet you in the car. I forgot to brush my teeth."

I trudge up the stairs, wavering between euphoria and exhaustion. I wash my face, brush my teeth and reapply deodorant, just in case. I also drink two glasses of water. I'm awake when I get to the car. I've been on the Post Road for a few minutes when she decides to poke me with a stick.

"Trevor wants to go out after the show tonight."

What?! I snap a look at her.

"Look out!" she squeals and I pull back into our lane before I can head-on a mail truck.

"Are you okay?" she asks.

"No. You cannot go out with Trevor." My face is hot with anger as my heart thumps wildly.

"Why not?"

"Because he's four years older than you."

"He's nice."

"No, Trevor is not nice. No, you're not going out with him."

"Why not?"

"Well, for one thing, he's dating Macaria Berber. You know that, right? For another, he's an adult and what he wants to do with you is a felony." Her eyes widen. "Third, he's a drug addict and a drunk." I pull into the town streets

and slow down. The parking lot is full, so I pull into a
parking spot on the curb.

"I think that's silly," she remarks.

"It doesn't matter. You're not going out with him."

"Not even in a group?"

"Not even in a group. Promise you won't ride with him
either."

She turns to me, her full lips pursed.

"That's funny." I fail to understand her point. She
sighs. "You're the one that nearly killed us this morning."

She gets out of the car and I sit there shaking for about
five minutes. I'm afraid to drive now that the full impact of
nearly crashing hits me and then Cheyenne pokes her head
out of the door and I decide to calm down by hanging out
with her. She's checking dancers in and trying to do pliés to
get ready for her rehearsal. Out of sheer silliness, I start to
emulate her moves. Of course, guys can't move like girls,
but I was a pretty good dancer only a couple of years ago,
so I don't do badly. Several of the mothers compliment me.
Cheyenne jokes I should be her partner tonight.

When the volume of dancers drops off, I tug her into
the bathroom off the lobby and cover her with kisses. I've
got my hand inside her leo and trying to figure out where to
put my other hand when the door at my back opens and
Mrs. Sim's stares at us in the mirror.

"Ms. Theriault, there is an entire company waiting
upon your presence." Cheyenne scrambles in the direction
she's supposed to have been five minutes ago, tucking
herself in as she goes, and I stand there with a rapidly-
deflating tent in my jeans. "You should go home now.
You're being a distraction." Mrs. Sims leaves me standing

there in the bathroom, well aware that I'm not only a distraction but an idiot. I straighten my clothes and ease some discomfort and then step out of the bathroom. She's not gone. Rebecca is teaching the class. Mrs. Sims is schooling me.

"How much did you have to drink this morning, Mr. Wyngate?" It's hard to read her British accent. She could be cold and biting or hoping I have a good day.

"I'm – uh - ." I have no excuse and I know it. Nailed to a wall under a magnifying glass.

"When you were one of my dancers, I was concerned for you. I am still concerned for you. You must be more careful than you are."

"Yes, ma'am."

"Are you alright to drive?"

"Yes, ma'am."

"Then you should go home now and consider what possessed you to drink this early in the morning. You'll need to answer your father because I intend to tell him about it. Good day to you."

Mrs. Sims and Helen Anderson are two people I can never lie to successfully. I leave my car at the curb and walk to the closest open coffee house to eat a bagel and drink the strongest Americano they've got. I take the circuitous route back to the studio to retrieve my car. I drive like an old lady back to the house and slip up to my room. I take the bottle back to the pantry. Then I go back upstairs and sit on my loveseat, reliving the momentary terror of the mail truck bearing down on us.

What the hell is wrong with me? I could have killed Alyse because I was distracted and driving with two full shots inside me – but I also got Cheyenne in trouble and – Mrs. Sims' words echo back at me. "I was concerned when I was your teacher and I am still concerned." I'm more concerned about that than I am that she's going to call my dad.

How did I get here?

I can't remember my first drink. The earliest one I remember was taking a sip of my mother's wine. In that memory, I know what it will taste like, so it wasn't my first sip. I'm in early elementary and she's allowing me sips of her wine.

I do remember the first time I drank hard liquor. The summer of the divorce, Dad hosted his annual summer soiree at the house. Ordinarily, Laren made all the arrangements and would have booked the country club or another venue, but Dad lost track of it and so hosted it at the house. I remember the caterers carrying in all the crates of booze and setting up tables, turning the kitchen into a restaurant, the foyer into a steam line, and the study and living room into a bistro that spilled out onto the terraces and a tent on the lawn. I'd been sad ever since Mom departed and I hated crowds of nosy adults even then, but I did my duty by escorting Alyse through the food line and letting people fawn over us before we made our escape upstairs.

Divorce disturbed my sleep and so I woke at dawn and went downstairs. The guests had departed of course, but they'd left all their drinks and I satisfied my curiosity by tasting all of the watered-down leavings. I remember it as the first time I knew Tilly was fully on my side because when she found me singing my heart out, she loaded me

into the car and drove me to the beach, let me stumble
around until I got uncoordinated and puked in the sand and
then took me home and let me sleep it off.

I felt like crap the rest of the day, but looking back, I'd
never felt more alive and comfortable in my skin than for
those couple of hours while the booze swirled in my
bloodstream. I felt happy for that little while – kind of like I
thought I was supposed to feel all the time. Soon after that,
whenever Dad would leave a drink unattended, I'd take a
deep swallow of it. If he noticed, he never said.

I danced in those days. Mrs. Sims worried about me
then. What if what was going on with me since I got back
from Europe had been going on all the way back then?

I wrap my arms around my knees and stare out the
window, shivering.

Fusion

Peter

I wake to a pounding on my door and then a hand shaking my shoulder. Tilly floats above me, dressed in evening clothes, her hair curled.

"You're going to be late for the performance."

"Not for a few more hours." I try to turn away. My head throbs dully.

"You've got an hour. I'm going now to meet your father and grandparents. You need to get showered and changed."

I look at my phone and sure enough, it's 6:00 pm. I fell asleep and took a four-hour nap. I roll off the loveseat and stumble into the shower. I don't usually get my hair wet more than once a day because all the product in the world won't overcome the frizz water causes, but I need it tonight. Maybe if I just don't shampoo it, it'll be okay. The headache retreats to just a spot behind my right eye. I pop a Tylenol, brush my teeth and grab dress clothes from the hangers in my closet. I brush the now-empty backpack and immediately regret having put the bottle back, but I don't have time to deal with it. I don't even have time to dry my hair to straighten it. I rub mousse in it and let it curl. I'm on the Post Road 20 minutes before the performance starts.

I can't find parking at Theater 4 where the performance is. I park on the street a block away and jog to the theater. They're closing the doors as I push through them, snagging a program as I flit past. I pause a moment, my eyes struggling to adjust to the low light. I could use my phone flashlight function, but that's just rude to the performer who is no doubt getting into position. I slide in along the back wall because I can't see any open seats.

A single spotlight in tight focus illuminates the lone dancer on the stage. Cheyenne holds the music-box-dancer stance until the audience is almost convinced she's a statue … and then the music starts. It's the actual song "Music Box Dancer" and her performance amazes. She's strong and agile, no tottering on pointe and she hits every beat. Halfway through the song, a hip hop version starts, and Trevor and another male dancer join her before the curtain. They're dressed in black and their bold moves seem jarring to her delicate pink ballerina, but soon she's matching them move for move. And then the curtain sweeps open and the company swirls around them, ballet dancers in pink and toe shoes and hip-hoppers in black. Cheyenne joins her group and the delicate song begins again, to the mock jeering of the hip-hoppers. Then Trevor steps forward and tries to go on pointe. You can manage pointe in hip-hop shoes and

Trevor is amazingly strong, but your body doesn't take the erect posture of a female on pointe. He copies them, pretends to fall, and then the hip-hop music interweaves with the Music Box Dancer and a hesitant Cheyenne joins him to do both. The ballet dancers' pair off with the hip-hoppers and they all move to the double arrangement.

Wow, I miss dancing!

Alyse is the lead in that ballet-jazz fusion number with Frank Sinatra. I haven't seen her perform since Christmas and the improvement is astonishing. A little bobble on a couple of moves is all – times when she has to adjust her feet slightly to keep her balance. Pointe is hard. It takes time to be as good as Cheyenne. She'll get there.

More numbers follow, each so absorbing I don't notice that I'm still standing or that my phone has three messages. At the intermission, I read through them.

ALAN – I can't believe you're missing your sister's performance.

"I'm not," I say as I join him, Granddad Mike and Lucy in their VIP seating. I hold up my phone to show I got his message. "I slipped in just as it started, so I stayed in the back."

Alan's face deliberately relaxes. Granddad Mike shows me the seat that was meant to be mine. I read my other messages.

CHEYENNE – You okay?

TREVOR – Does your sister know you don't want her dating me?

PETER – *Mrs. Sims is right, and we know it. Are YOU okay?*

I doubt I'll hear from her until later. Cells weren't allowed backstage when I danced.

PETER – *Doesn't matter what she knows. You go out with her and I'm going to hurt you.*

Macaria passes me trailed by a girl about Alyse's age who looks somewhat like Macaria. I didn't know Mac had a sister. I smile at her because it's the right thing to do.

"I need something cold to drink," Lucy says. "Maybe we could go up to the reception area."

Dad exchanges glances with the two suited men with him and they imperceptibly shake their heads. Security ruins everything.

"I'm going to take my bride up for some of that punch." Granddad Mike nods his head at me and cuts his eyes, so I know he's hoping I'll stay and talk to Alan. I smile back. I'm so on edge right now that I hate the idea of the crowd that is no doubt forming out in the foyer but hanging out with Alan also makes me nervous. I opt for it only because Granddad Mike wants me to.

"Mrs. Sims sent me a message at the beginning of the performance asking me to speak with her after the performance. Do you know what that might be about? Has Alyse gotten herself in trouble?"

"She wouldn't be performing if she'd gotten into trouble, Dad." I'm frankly surprised Cheyenne is still performing. Mrs. Sims is a dragon about starting on time. "She probably wants to talk to you about funding. She's planning her retirement and she wants Dance Theater to continue. She was telling me something about setting up a non-profit."

"I would be glad to help her with that. Thank you for bringing it to my attention."

I nod, secretly hoping it distracts Mrs. Sims from telling him that I was drunk this morning. It's the right thing to do, letting him know that she needs something he can supply. My need to stay out of trouble doesn't mean I can't do something good, right?

My phone vibrates.

> CHEYENNE – I'm fine. She blamed you, gave me a lecture about professionalism. Are you in trouble?

> PETER – *I don't think she's told my dad yet, but it'll be okay. I screwed up.*

> CHEYENNE – I was the one with the obligation to show up on time.

> TREVOR – I don't want to date her. She's too young. Maybe you need to calm down a little.

> PETER – *I'm warning you.*

"Who are you talking to?" Alan's frowning again.

"Friends. I see the Andersons. I should go say hello."

He nods. It must suck to not be allowed to wander around. I fail to see why not. We're in a friendly environment, filled with people who came to see a ballet performance. Really? How dangerous could they be?

"Pete," Helen greets as I approach. Her husband John gives me a big smile and squeezes my shoulder. My Tylenol is starting to wear off, but the hangover I so richly deserve isn't that bad. "You need to come over tomorrow, continue telling us about your trip."

The night we had barbecue, John pumped me for details of my trip and I managed to come up with enough parent-approved adventures to satisfy them, but they want more. I'm pretty sure I've exhausted the well, forcing me to make stuff up. Ben appears at my elbow.

"Can I talk to you for a second?"

We step away from his parents and put our heads together.

"Have you dealt with the designated driver need for the party? Trevor ended up with three people busted for DUI. Wouldn't want to break your perfect record."

"Vic and Tilly usually handle that. She said they would." I'd kind of forgotten about the party. If I was going to be more sensible about drinking, I'd need to do it there too. "You got any volunteers?"

"Pamela and me, yeah, but she won't hang around if things get really ridiculous."

"That's Trevor's parties, not mine."

"I'm just saying. That one you had in the spring – you got really stupid and kind of lost control of it."

"I learned my lesson. No drinking games with Finn."

The dark hole between that fourth shot of bourbon and waking up in the hospital still scares me, but not as much as the mail truck this morning. Ben's forehead puckers. What should I say?

"You know, you don't have to do this," Ben says. "If you canceled, nobody would hold it against you. You probably should have canceled the one in the spring."

Ben doesn't know about my ER visit, but he knew about Uncle Matthew and he knows I got really drunk. A fleeting thought flits through my brain. This party is a worse idea. But, of course, I can't say that. I can't disappoint my friends. It's probably the last time we'll all get together. I just have to resolve to keep it to one or two beers. I can do that.

The lights flicker to let us know the intermission is drawing to a close. I tell Ben the party is on and move toward my seat. The second half is better than the first and after, Dad talks to Mrs. Sims while I congratulate Alyse on her great performance. She leans into my hug then rushes off to congratulate some friends on their performances. I'm worried about what Mrs. Sims might be telling Alan but she, Rebecca and he are all smiling. I follow Alyse, turning aside to where Trevor and Cheyenne are standing surrounded by adoring teenyboppers.

"Are we good?" Trevor asks.

"Just accept that she's too young for you."

"Why would I waste time breaking in a flat-chested little girl when I can have Mac whenever I want?"

He's got a point. Cheyenne puts her arm around my back.

"That opening number – WOW!"

"Yeah. I'm pretty amazed at how well it turned out."

"I'm sorry I almost got you suspended from it."

"Stop. I knew what time it was, and I should have been responsible. My parents are coming. You might want to duck away before they realize."

I hate that my dad means I can't meet her parents, but I nod sharply and step over to congratulate someone else on their performance. These are my people – dancers. I'm still halfway thinking I should look into dance classes in Hartford.

Time for that tomorrow. In the meantime, I've got a party to plan and people to congratulate. And an angry father to quell – most likely.

I'm talking to Granddad Mike and Lucy when Dad is ready to go.

"Where's Alyse?" I ask.

"She caught a ride home with Tilly," Dad assures me. "I'm hoping you'll ride with me."

"I brought my car, but I can walk with you to yours."

Dad looks at the security team and we all move toward the exit. I'm waiting for the hammer to come down and surprised that he isn't frowning.

"Mrs. Sim said it was your idea to talk to me about funding for the non-profit."

"Yeah."

"I've always supported Dance Theater and I'm pleased to help them with the transition. Rebecca was with Joffrey Ballet for six and a half years and another six and a half with a big illusionist show in Las Vegas. She's very professional. Mrs. Sims would transition into retirement and there'd be a board created to continue the theater. It's a very good idea. I just wanted to tell you that."

I breathe a sigh of relief, amazed that I'm not in trouble when he leans in just as we reach his car.

"Cool the cocktails before breakfast." His whisper is like a gentle breeze. "You got away with that in Europe and I'm sure Collin encouraged it. It's not legal here. Got it?"

We match gazes and I nod. He smiles and claps me on the shoulder before getting in the backseat. I can't believe I got away with it. I'm relieved and – and another feeling that I can't identify and that inexplicably scares me to death.

After Party

Cheyenne

The after-party is in full swing and I'm looking around for Peter, wondering where he might be when I see Alyse standing with Ben. I don't expect Alyse to tell me where Peter might be, but I think Ben and I are friendly after Splish Splash, so when Alyse flits away in dragonfly fashion through the crowd, I approach Ben.

"Hey."

"Hi. Have you seen Peter?"

"No. I don't think he's here. I haven't seen him."

"He's come to other after-parties."

"Sure, but he asked me to be Alyse's escort."

"Deliberately?"

"I think he might still be feeling a little jetlagged. Or something. He just asked me if I'd escort her."

"I just thought – he sort of said he'd be here."

"Pete usually doesn't miss parties, but --." He shrugs as Alyse floats back to stand beside him.

"Is Peter still not feeling well?" I ask her.

She raises an eyebrow.

"Considering what happened this morning – maybe not so well."

She slides her gaze sideways toward Ben, which I take to mean he doesn't know. I excuse myself and climb the stairs to the second floor to use the phone. Peter doesn't answer, so I text him.

CHEYENNE – *Missing you at the after-party. Are you sure you're okay?*

I don't get an immediate answer, so I go back to the party. Trevor is talking much louder than he should. God, is he ever sober?

Macaria grins at me.

"Where's Peter?"

"Question of the night. Alyse says he went home. You here with Trevor?"

"I wish I weren't. I'm the designated driver. What a shitty job!"

"Since when does Trevor think he needs a designated driver?"

"Since what happened the other day with Pete and his boat. He tried to tell us he shouldn't drink before piloting the boat. Trevor and I fought about it and he declared me the designated driver."

"Sounds like you lost that fight."

"Kind of, but he's fun to hang out with and he's leaving next week, so ...."

Trevor realizes she's not with him and comes to sweep her into a sexy kiss. I sigh. My phone vibrates.

PETER – I'm staying home tonight. The after-parties kind of get on my nerves. Too many young kids. See you tomorrow night.

If he weren't such a delicious guy, I think I might go see who else I could kiss right now. Instead, I return to the party to make small talk and be congratulated on heading to Joffrey. I should feel happy that I'm leaving as a success, but I feel lonely even in a crowd of people. I'm not getting attached. I'm not. But....

Decisions at Dawn

Peter

I wake before dawn, having tossed and turned half the night. I'm not going back to sleep, so I don a sweatshirt over my loungers and tennis shoes and head out to the back yard, down the switchback stairs to the beach. I remember when we heard that Uncle Matthew had died. I came down here and bawled my eyes out, shouting at the surf until I was hoarse.

The funeral was two days later. Uncle Matthew had been areligious and he had no family interested in planning his funeral. Granddad Mike and Lucy had taken on the honor. St. Matthews Episcopal Church could seat a few hundred. Matthew's friends looked strange in the cerebral chilliness of a high-liturgical church – New York City musicians, artists, and hotel managers just weren't familiar with churches any more than I was. They filled half the pews. Flowers from a good many more filled the rest of the church. Meanwhile, Mom chose not to come and their parents didn't even send flowers.

Dad explained that Uncle Matthew had been a great guy – why he'd kept him as a brother-in-law even after getting rid of Laren – but his earlier playboy existence alienated his biological family and he'd not tried to re-establish contact after he got sober. His "family" was an odd collection of friends, coworkers, and people he'd helped over the years. Granddad Mike spoke of him as a phoenix who had risen from the ashes. I marveled that I had known so little about him. He'd seemed happy and energetic that day on the island. And too soon, he'd been sick and dying, then dead.

In retrospect, I should have canceled my party set for the following weekend. I felt like crap and getting drunk was the only thing that made it better. Finn's stupid drinking game made everything else fade away. It almost made me fade away … for good.

Out on the east, the sky cracks with a single line of dark blue in the black. I stuff my cold hands in my underarms and settle down on the sand to watch the show.

What if I gave a party and didn't show up? Probably can't do that. No, I just need to stick with non-alcoholic beverages early in the evening and maybe one or two beers later – and then just stop. I watch as a wink of green replaces the blue. It'll be the last party of a successful run – about five times a year since I got back from boarding school. The cops never show up, the only one who ever threw up on the carpet was me after the guests went home. Everybody had fun. And, maybe I'll finally get lucky. I remember to remind Tilly to lock Dad's suite. In the spring, before I got wasted with Finn, I had to chase people out of Dad's rooms.

The green is bleeding up into the black when a slice of gold narrows my eyes to a slit. I noticed Tilly had stocked the guest rooms with condoms. It's neither of our business, but nobody wants my father to be named as an accessory in a paternity suit. Maybe this party isn't a good idea.

The wind ruffles my hair as the lower sky blushes pink and the reticulated clouds glow a deep purple. I never heard her steps on the sand, so I'm slightly startled when Alyse settles down beside me.

"Gorgeous." Her voice holds awe, like the reverence you might give in church or the public library. I grunt. There are tears on my cheeks and I don't know why or even remember crying them. "You okay?"

"Yeah."

"About yesterday --."

"It won't happen again."

"You mean yelling at me for teasing you about Trevor?"

"It's not funny. He's too old for you." She nods her gaze, on the sunrise. The sky behind the purple clouds is now mauve. "But that's not – I did something stupid yesterday and I won't do it again. I'm sorry I scared you."

She doesn't say anything. We sit there watching the sky turn blue. Finally, I stand up. My face feels like it's breaking out in zits. I need a shower and breakfast.

"She didn't come." I pause in turning. "She never comes."

"Yeah. But Dad did, even though it was probably a feat to arrange."

"Why does she hate me?"

I lick my lips. I don't know what to say. I've never understood Laren. I can't excuse her behavior or explain it away.

"I don't know what to say. But I love you and Dad does. And whether you believe it or not, Tilly does too. And, Mrs. Sims and Rebecca obviously think you have talent – which you do, by the way. Why Laren doesn't want to be a parent to us – that's a mystery I can't solve."

She wipes tears off her cheeks and reaches for my hand. I pull her to her feet.

"She loves you, though."

I look deeply into her blue eyes.

"Not exactly. It's a lot more complicated than that."

She doesn't understand and I won't tell her. I can hardly tell myself. I turn back toward the stairs.

"Ella's moving. I'm going to be all alone here when you leave."

"You need to make some new friends, then. I need to take a shower. How about we go to breakfast together – just you and me?"

She puts her arm around my back and we walk up the stairs together.

Party

Ben

I never knew how Pete pulled it off, but with a few short days and some phone calls, he's transformed his house into party central and somehow gotten the adults to leave. Tilly and Vic aren't far away. They'll be providing rides later in the evening. Pete's been doing this ever since he got back from boarding school at the end of 10th grade and he pulls it off so seamlessly that nobody else can even come close. Trevor sometimes holds epic parties but there are always issues. Earlier in the summer, he attempted to make up for Pete's absence over the 4th of July and the neighbors called the cops. Pete really has no near neighbors, but I sometimes wonder if he bribes the local patrol officers. These days it could just be that the local cops don't want to embarrass the governor, but Alan Wyngate had only been running for office when Peter started this.

The biggest issue is always parking. The circular drive at Wyngate House is huge, but Pete's guests always exceed capacity. I don't want to get trapped when it's time to drive people home, so I park my car across the road on the edge of the woods. Wouldn't surprise me if Governor Wyngate owns this property too.

Pete and Trevor are the only ones in the front foyer when I enter. They're discussing the playlist. Trevor already holds a beer in one hand but Pete looks stone-cold sober and is actually drinking a flavored seltzer water. He hates vodka, so I have to wonder what clear liquor is mixed with the bubbles.

"I'm telling you – JoE is charting."

"I don't get it. It's all rhythm, not music. It's fine if that's what you want to play, but mix it up a little."

Trevor laughs.

"Unfortunately, I can't scratch platters like they used to in the 90s, but yeah – I get it. There will be a mix."

"Hey, Ben. What do you think?"

Pete hands me a playlist. I don't know half the songs. Trevor has wide tastes, which is why Pete asks him to DJ. There's always something for everyone. Andy Harmon and his sister Regina come in, setting down a keg of beer. There's already four waiting, but the attitude is that you can never have too much beer.

"Man, you should have some," Trevor encourages. "Take the edge off before everybody gets here."

Pete does seem a little uptight tonight, but the last thing he needs is beer. It's a long night ahead and I've come to realize that Pete can't hold his liquor as well as he pretends.

"I'm going to go easy tonight, Trevor. Last time, Tilly wasn't happy when I got drunk and couldn't keep things in control. So, this time, I'm going to go slow."

Good for him. Trevor makes a face and drains his beer, tossing the bottle in a nearby trash barrel. Macaria Berber comes in from somewhere, kissing him. She remarks about the beer on his lips and he gets two bottles so they can be taste-bud twins.

Speaking of bud, Viggo Martini just arrived. I liked pot for about a semester until Pete got busted with it on campus and then I pretty much stopped smoking it altogether. I nibble an occasional edible. I won't tonight since I've agreed to be a designated driver. I fear Pam won't show up. She has a bad feeling about this party. So far, it seems pretty tame for one of Pete's shindigs, but she's never been to one and the idea that there are no adults on-site seems dangerous to her. It could go that way if Pete gets distracted.

Alyse comes floating down the stairs in this striking red dress with a diaphanous skirt that is way too short. Pete cuts his gaze that way and his mouth tightens, but he doesn't confront her. Maybe he's already had the conversation or maybe he's given up. When she tries to take a beer, he puts a hand on her wrist.

"That's the only one you'll be allowed tonight, so you'd better time it for the maximum fun."

"You were limited to one beer a night when you were my age?"

"I wasn't a 100-pound girl and Ben used to try and tap my brakes all the time. It's my party. You follow my rules."

She makes a face and flounces across the room.
Flounces is not a word I use often, but it suits her body
language. I'm surprised Pete remembers those bygone days
of hanging out at the lake and my suggesting he stick to two
or three beers. In those pre-boarding school days, he
sometimes actually listened, though not as well as I would
have liked.

Pamela wears a champaign-colored tunic over leggings
and looks ready to dance, which few people are actually
doing. It's tough to start the party especially until people are
a little drunk, so I'm not moving with the music until more
people get here. Cheyenne's wearing a dark blue off-one-
shoulder dress that showcases her dancer legs. Alyse talks
with Macaria's little sister, sipping from a red solo cup. The
notorious anti-carb stance of most dancers limits the drink
selection. Maybe she's wisely chosen water.

The foyer begins to fill up and spill into the other
rooms and even up the stairs. Viggo disappears. I figure he's
outside selling his supply. Pete doesn't like pot, but he's not
narrow-minded on the subject, so he won't cater it, but he
doesn't object to it outdoors.

Pete sweeps Cheyenne into his arms and they move out
onto the officially designated dance floor, which will soon
be any room you can stand. Pete and Cheyenne move like
they've been dancing together for a decade and maybe they
have been. They were in the same dance studio and I never
paid much attention to it then. Pete hasn't forgotten how to
dance and she takes her choreography from him. Others
begin to filter onto the dance floor and eventually Pamela
and I join them.

I'm hot and need some water when she announces she needs to go to the restroom. I crack a cap on a bottle of water and drain half of it in a single swig. The music pounds my ears, but I can hear cheering in the study. Pete always locks up the bar before we get here. He's smart enough to know his father will object to teenagers hitting his expensive booze. Pete appears at my elbow and drains a bottle of water before grabbing a second one.

"How you doing?" I ask.

"Hot. You?"

That's a sure sign he's not drinking yet. He still cares if I'm having a good time.

"Also hot. Dancing is exercise."

"Cheyenne makes me look good." A raucous bellow sounds from the study. "What's going on in there?"

I don't know, so we go together. A group of guys kneel around the coffee table, hooting and hollering as Finn Conover plays quarters with Ian Rice. I tried that once and never will again. Pete leans back against the bar front and watches. He swallows tightly. Is he thirsty even with a bottle of water in his hand? This thing is about to go south if he is.

"I'm out," Ian announces. He wobbles to his feet. "Gotta go puke now."

"Bathroom," Pete commands, pointing. Ian stumbles in the direction he's pushed in.

"Hey, the reigning champion," Finn hails. "You owe me a rematch."

Pete hesitates, licking his lips and I hold my breath. Yeah, I want him to have a good time, but pouring Pete into bed after one of these parties is getting old.

Quarters

Peter

I almost say 'yes', but they're playing quarters with scotch, which always upsets my stomach. I drain about a quarter of the water bottle to buy myself time. Fortunately, Trevor comes dancing in from the foyer and announces he wants a piece of Finn, who hesitates.

"The challenge is for Pete."

"I've got a party to host," I tell him. Ben's trying not to look at me, but when I say that he cuts me a sharp glance. Maybe I'm surprising people tonight. That's a good thing, right?

Where'd my date go? I head back to the foyer where Alyse and Macaria both appear to be dancing with the same guy. Whatever is in that red solo cup had better be non-alcoholic. Ben touches my shoulder.

"You had me worried for a second in there."

"It's way too early to get that wasted." He smiles at me like when I learned to ride a bike and then moves off to dance with Pamela again. We're at the halfway mark now, so I fill a solo cup from the best keg and work my way through the crowd sipping the first beer I'm allowing myself tonight. I'll have another around 10 so I'm sober enough to drive people home when they start getting obnoxious around 2:00 am. The beer relaxes my shoulders as I climb the stairs looking for Cheyenne. She's already had a couple of beers and I worry about leaving her alone. Guys will be guys when there's a drunk chick around.

The guest powder room off the hall is large enough for a party of its own and it's living up to its name. Viggo nods at me from behind the mirror he's set on the table. Damn! Cocaine? I never saw that coming. I also never thought I'd see Cheyenne leaning over the mirror with a straw up one nostril.

"Hey, Pete. The first hit's free for the host." Viggo should know better. Drugs don't interest me – never have. And coke – that sounds like bipolar manic to me and I am not going to be my mom.

Cheyenne turns around, her face flushed but still sexy. She purrs as she reaches for me.

"You would enjoy it."

No, I wouldn't. I tried Adderall junior year, around the same time I tried pot, though not the same day. The Adderall made the whole world seem to be moving too slow for me. I could hear the bright quick voice of my mother coming out of my mouth. Like I said – I won't be her.

I toss my empty beer cup in the trash as hanging onto it tempts me to refill it. Cheyenne wraps her arms around me.

"Give it a try." That's a challenge, but I'm not taking it up any more than I took up Finn's. I lean into her ear.

"You know about my mom?"

I told her about my mom that day when we shopped for jeans. She pulls her head back so we can meet gazes, but she's perplexed. My god, woman, can you not understand that I might be a little afraid of setting off something that's a lifelong problem?

"You're being a party pooper."

Maybe. I've never done one of these parties trying to stay sober. There's a bottle of vodka being passed around, but no unclaimed cups in evidence, so I grab it and take a nice long swallow of it. I pass it on. Cheyenne unbuttons my shirt. I allow it. Someone stumbles into my back and laughs, waving a bottle around.

"Oh, coke. Here, hold this." The guy wanders over to the mirrored table and I take a slug of his bottle before I kiss Cheyenne. Ah, bourbon, come here, my lovely.

Cheyenne tugs on me and we go out to the hallway. My room has three couples in it, but a guy with unzipped pans and a girl with messy hair vacate the guest room across the hall. I lock the door behind us. Cheyenne sprawls back on the bed, her hands splayed across the woven fabric of the upholstered headboard. I drain the bourbon to the last drop and climb on top of her.

Designated Driver

Ben

The beat of the music interferes with my heart rate as I try to assess just how drunk Alyse might be. She's loud, flushed and uncharacteristically uncoordinated as she dances to a hip-hop song I don't know and never want to hear again.

"Hey, hey, you probably need to go lie down," I tell her. Her room was locked the last I checked. Alyse has seen enough of Pete's parties to know that her room needs to be sealed for its safety. I don't know how I'm supposed to get her into it. I need to find Pete and have him text Vic and Tilly because things are going south now. Finn shouts from the study that he won at killing the most brain cells. I think it's round two between him and Trevor, which Trevor has lost. He's puking in the bushes. Not to be outdone, so is Macaria.

239

Meanwhile, I'm looking for Pete. I'm beginning to think he's in hiding when I encounter Viggo coming out of a bathroom on the second floor.

"I haven't seen him for about an hour. He didn't want to partake of the party favors, so he and that dancer chick took a bottle somewhere."

Damn. I'm not surprised, but I had hoped. It's up to me to call in the cavalry. Fortunately, I have Tilly's number in my phone from sometimes when she called me trying to track him down.

"I'm at the bottom of the drive." She sounds like this is everyday normal. Not for the first time, I wonder how she gets away with allowing Pete's behavior. Does his father have no knowledge of what goes on here? Or is he aware and thinks she has it handled? Mom doesn't think she does and I'm beginning to agree with her. "Vic has already taken some people home. Just start shooing others toward the door. It helps if you turn off the music."

After I create something resembling silence – sending Alyse toward the nearest garbage can to puke -- I go out to the terrace to drag Macaria and Trevor to their feet. On our way through the study, I see Finn has passed out on the floor. I meet Pamela in the foyer.

"Can you take these two home? I'll get Finn before he wakes up and decides to drink some more and needs the Emergency Room."

"They're going to puke in my car."

"Keep the windows rolled down and you brought bags, right?"

She makes a face. I'm an experienced designated driver, but I remember that feeling my first time. My car had already been broken in ... by me when Pete had to drive us back from a beach party after I drank too much. He might have had a learner's permit and I now wonder just how drunk he might have been.

I walk down the driveway with her, keeping Trevor moving while she herds Macaria. Trevor's so drunk he's proclaiming his love of me and he can't even put on his seatbelt. Macaria's running mascara makes her look like a pretty racoon, but she's less wasted than Trevor ... or maybe more used to being that wasted. She hiccups and apologizes to Pamela for being a mess.

Tilly has a carful, but she stops and asks me if I know where Pete is.

"I lost track of him about an hour ago." A shadow crosses her face. "He was still sober then."

"Well, that's good." She glances toward the house. "If you find him, tell him to text me."

"Yes, ma'am. Alyse is drunk, by the way."

"I put the key to her room in the drawer to the left of the dishwasher." That news doesn't surprise her at all. Did she just not trust Peter's ability to keep his sister sober or does she just think it's normal?

"I'll take care of it."

Alyse curls up on the flagstone floor of the foyer, so I must pick her up. She's completely wasted, so she's floppy. Thank goodness she weighs about 90 pounds. The party crowd clumsily sorts itself out now that the music is off. Jason McAllister stopped drinking a few hours into the party because he can do that. He's rounding up people to drive home. I almost wish I could snag a beer as my reward for doing this, but I know how that would look if I got pulled over, so I don't.

I deposit Alyse in her bed, placing her body pillow behind her back so she isn't at risk of choking if she throws up. Pete's room is deserted. I chase people out of a couple of the guest rooms, though one is locked. There's no noise when I knock. I go back downstairs, lift Finn in a fireman's carry and head for my car. Andy and his sister are leaning against it. I tell them to get in and I leave with a full car.

Curve

Cheyenne

The banging hardly registered except as annoying. I was snuggled into the pillow and didn't even protest. A little while later, I wake because of the silence. After hours of laughter and music, the quiet screams. Pete shifts beside me. His face is flushed and his lips slightly parted as he sleeps. I roll on top of him, fumbling with the open zipper on his jeans. Why'd he put his pants back on? His eyes open, confused.

"What time is it?" he mumbles, blinking at the room. He shifts under me until he can fish his phone out of his pocket. "Two-thirty. Crap. Tilly's going to kill me."

Two-thirty? My folks are going to be pissed. I'm 18, so they can't give me a curfew anymore, but they extracted a promise from me that I'd be home by two or call. That's okay. We'll work it out. I should get home before they notice.

"I gotta go."

Pete pushes me off, then sits on the side of the bed, rubbing a hand through his hair. He doesn't stumble on the way to the bathroom to wash his face. I watch in the mirror as he drinks two glasses of water one right after another, then washes the glass and brings it to me.

"You're going to want that. Helps you not be so hungover."

My hands shake as I take it. The room feels like it's moving on an incoming tide. Pete glances at his phone.

"Vic's taking another carload and he says Tilly won't be back for a while. You need to wait."

"For what?"

"One of them to drive you. I need fresh air."

I lean into him for a kiss, but he moves away from me, heads into the hallway. He pauses at a door and opens it, then closes it without a sound. Seriously? He leaves my bed to check on his sister? He wasn't a bad lover. Clearly inexperienced. Way too quick. The coke meant I didn't care if he fulfilled my needs, but yeah – typical guy. Fell asleep as soon as he was satisfied. I can imagine spending time with him if we weren't going different ways in a couple of weeks – if he weren't hung up on his sister.

The house is a mess, but there's hardly anyone left here – a few people passed out on couches and a catering staff starting to do the cleanup. Pete steers me away from them into the driveway.

"Which is your car?" he asks.

I got here early, so parked my Nissan in the circle. We can easily drive out now. I drop my keys and stumble trying to pick them up. Stupid high heels. He bends for the keys as if he didn't drink a half a bottle of bourbon.

"That's sexy, a guy who can hold his liquor."

"I didn't mean to do that," he mumbles. He leans against my car.

"I gotta get home. My parents are going to be pissed."

"Vic's still a half-hour out. It's a nice night. Relax."

"No, I've got to go. You can drive me home and Vic can pick you up at my house."

"I've had a lot to drink, Cheyenne."

"You already got me in trouble with Rebecca and Mrs. Sims. My parents are already not happy I'm dating a Republican. Don't do this."

"I'm not a Republican. Not old enough to register yet." He frowns at the car.

"I'll drive myself." I try to grab the keys from him. He pulls them back. He's tall, so it's not hard for him to keep them from me. "I don't want to spend the last couple of weeks home in the doghouse." I drop my purse and he bends to collect the contents.

"Are you going to make me walk?"

He frowns at me, blinking as if he's got something in his eyes.

"There shouldn't be much traffic. I'll take you."

We get in and he adjusts the seat to his height. Kid has long legs. He puts on his seatbelt and waits for me to do the same. He drives conservatively – old lady style. The breeze in my face perks me up. I ask him about our next date. He's slow to answer, blinking at the road, then yawning.

"Yeah, we'll talk about that tomorrow. Maybe the day after since you're going to have a hell of a hangover in the morning."

"Me? What about you?"

"I have a lot of practice at this." He does. I laugh. He laughs. He focuses on the road, turning on the air conditioning even though the windows are down.

The Post Road would be the direct path through town to my house, but he stays on Elmwood.

"Why this way? It takes longer."

"Not as likely to get pulled over for DUI." He's pissed at me?

"You're not that drunk."

"I shouldn't be driving. You could have waited for Vic."

We drive in silence after that. He's blinking rapidly, adjusting himself in the seat frequently. The air conditioner puts out arctic air. This part of Elmwood goes through a private reserve. A sign reminds me of a favorite spot.

"You ever make out at Carson's Point?"

"Nope." He rubs a hand over his face, frowning. Even at three in the morning with a half-bottle of bourbon in him, he's sexy and so damn handsome. Forget my parents.

"I bet you've never had sex in the front seat of a car." I'd bet tonight was his first time, judging by his struggles with the condom. "Let's go in."

"I'm – uh --."

I unbuckle to reach for him. He swerves. There's a jolt like he hit something and the tires squeal.

"Cut it out!" he yells. "Put your seatbelt --. Shit!"

I turn forward as the car scrapes past the guardrail at the curve and then there's the tree.

Rude Awakening

Peter

I can't breathe. I float in cold darkness, trying to draw a breath. Urgent voices speak in my ear, but they make no sense as the world flashes red and white and then goes black.

I wake to alternating bars of light and hurried voices shouting what sounds like urgent information. My head throbs with every light I pass under. I close my eyes and sink back into darkness.

Breathing hurts as I gasp for each snatch of air. Light invades my closed eyelids, searing throbbing pain through my head. I protest weakly at the foul smell that fills my nose.

"Peter, can you open your eyes, please?"

I don't want to. It hurts too much. I don't know this man and I don't want to.

"Peter, open your eyes."

I drag my eyelids upward. My vision twists ominously and my stomach turns. I close them again.

"Open your eyes, Peter."

I try, but they won't stay open. On the third effort, I focus on a light-haired man in a white coat leaning over me.

"What is your name?"

I should be glad he provided it for me, although it would still be my name anyway.

"What year is it?"

I have to work that one out, but the answer only takes a second.

"Do you know where you are?"

It hurts to move my eyes, but yeah, this is a hospital. The smell of antiseptic roils my stomach, warning me to close my eyes again. My head now pounds in rhythm to the stabbing in my chest and about at the same intensity. Hands lift and move me. Scared and in pain, I cry out. I lay there a bit trying to breathe as shallowly as possible until I hear a voice I recognize. Dad?

When they slip an IV into my vein, the pain of the needle hardly registers against all the rest. All the pains mysteriously retreat.

"Concussion … separated shoulder … bruises … cracked ribs."

"Thank you, doctor. May I have a moment with him?"

I feel the others leave. The medicine would help me sleep after Dad talks. The hand on my shoulder sends a surging jolt of pain through my whole body. I open my eyes to look into my father's face. Alan looks stressed, his perfectly coifed hair mussed.

"How are you feeling?" he asks.

"Hurts." I can barely whisper. Alan's expression worries me. "Alyse okay?"

"Alyse wasn't in the car, Peter."

"Car?" I don't remember a car.

"Not exactly sure how you ended up driving it, but you ran into a tree."

"Tree?"

A long silence greets the question. My body no longer hurts and my head feels unfocused, fuzzy as a dandelion gone to seed.

"Do you remember driving Cheyenne Theriault's car?"

I shake my head, which makes the room twist and heave, forcing me to close my eyes against the dizziness.

"She's in ICU, Peter. You thoroughly screwed up this time."

"What? I don't—I don't remember driving."

Breathing hurt not just my ribs, but the actual passage of air into my lungs. A nurse replaces Alan and holds a mask to my nose and mouth. My ribs ease from the spasm and I feel the medication drag me down into the bed. Cheyenne? I hope she'll be okay. Driving her car? That seems unlikely. Where were we that I'd be driving her car instead of mine? I try to remember, but the drugs pull me down into sleep and I can't try anymore.

Battered & Bruised

Ben

It's late afternoon before I leave the Theriaults to visit Pete. There's no one waiting outside his room, so I just slip in through the partially open door. The purple and black bruising obscure his features. I'm not sure I'd recognize him if I didn't know him. I'm beyond mad at my best friend. Cheyenne is in critical condition and I want to punch Pete in the mouth for causing that, but my heart goes mushy to see him so beat up.

I'm about to turn and leave when he stirs, angling his head so he can see me from the eye that's not swollen shut.

"Ben." His voice slurs. "Whattimeit?"

"Mid-afternoon."

"Thirshy."

I don't move as he looks around for the cup of water that's probably not in his peripheral vision because his eye is swollen shut. He swallows noisily.

"Cheyenne," he mumbles. "Acshident."

An accident?

"You were drunk." My best friend – the guy I've spent part of almost every day with since I was six. He's a drunk.

"Didn't drink that much."

Anger forces the red-hot words out of my mouth.

"Bull shit! People saw you down half-a-bottle of bourbon. You were drunk."

"Why's I driving her car?"

"It doesn't matter. She's really hurt and when you have a wreck when you've been drinking, it's no accident."

His sole eye closes and he smiles like it's a nice dream he's having … while Cheyenne fights for her life one floor down.

"Pete." He doesn't react to the sound of his name. I'm done. I don't have anything more to say.

Intervention

Peter

I drift in and out of sleep, my head feeling like a balloon and my legs going numb. Occasionally, my stomach turns ominously. Other times I float in a dream, on my back in a bay. Uncle Matthew appears in front of me.

"Hey, wake up, kid." We climb the trail to the house. I try to interpret his expression. "Wow! What a treasure!"

I don't remember most of what we talked about that day, but the email he sent me comes to mind.

> **MATT - Life in the fast lane can end your life, kid. Don't do what I did. Choose to live longer.**

It's like we're standing on the beach with my sailboat Clotilde behind him and he's saying the words....

...and then my hand explodes in pain. I drag my eyes open as a doctor I don't recognize loops the IV tube over the pole and rolling it back from the bed. The liquid in the bag is only half gone. I'm confused.

"Can you feel the bed yet?"

Everything has this weird glow around it and the doctor's voice seems to echo from afar. I drift on the tide for several more minutes and then my body touches the bed and I become aware of my shoulder – not that it hurts, but that it could.

"You awake?" the doctor asks.

"Yeah. I'm probably going to need that stuff, right?"

"Not a good idea for you. Anything feel-good is a bad idea for you."

"What the --?"

"Dr. Tim Shaefer. We've met before. You want some water?"

He holds the cup while I suck from the straw. The fog clears a bit. I thank him, though a quiet throb pulses in my shoulder, still held back by the barrier of the now-withdrawn medication, but promising agony soon enough.

"So, before you feel the pain, we need to have a conversation."

"About?"

"Do you remember me from May?" I do remember my May emergency room visit, but mostly just the discomfort of having my stomach pumped. Did I sleep over? Was Schaefer there then? Maybe. "I told your step-mother then that you needed help. I see you didn't get any and now you're risking other lives. What were you doing before the accident?"

Accident? I remember waking up to the bright lights of the ER. Before that? I was choosing to stay sober with Ben before the party started. But wait, did I drink beer?

"There was a party." I'm pretty sure there was.

"How much did you drink?"

I think I remember a beer – a cup from a keg -- but I really don't even remember the party.

"I don't know."

"I bet you felt like Superman until a moment before you drove into the tree."

"I --." My stomach turns ominously. "Tree?"

"I'm not surprised you don't remember. Your BAC was more than twice the legal limit, which explains the hepatitis. Your bilirubin level is elevated, liver swollen. That's not a good sign. A lot of people, alcohol is their kryptonite."

"What do you know about it?" I whisper.

"I know nobody your age has that capacity without some practice."

It requires an explanation, but I'm not firing on all cylinders.

"We spent the summer in Europe."

"Yeah, that's a sprint and could explain the hepatitis. Still, you've been training for a marathon. When did you start drinking? Twelve – thirteen?" Twelve, but I don't say it aloud. "You don't have to answer, but you know the truth. You keep bottles hidden so you don't run short?" How does he know? "You need a little sip to study?"

I swear at him. I'm no different than any of my friends. Yeah, I have a beer occasionally. So what?

"Yeah, you thought kryptonite made you strong until you ran into the tree, and now you're scared. And that's good because if you keep going this way, you're going to end up a grease spot on the Long Island Expressway."

"No." My voice comes out so soft even I'm not convinced.

"You'll heal from these injuries, but your friend's going to need multiple surgeries to reconstruct her face. Next time someone might die."

"There won't be a next time." I wince as my ribs move from the force of my denial.

"Not if you quit drinking, no, but if you don't learn from this – yeah." A shiver runs through me, making me gasp against the pain. "You don't have to do it alone. You're getting out of the hospital tomorrow, but there's a meeting here at the hospital tonight, people who can help you. You could go down in a wheelchair or I could send someone up to talk with you. And, I've already spoken to your father. If you tell him you want to go to rehabilitation, I think he'd let you go."

"Or I could just not drink."

"Easy to say when the edge has been taken off by morphine." He pauses and I refuse to answer. "I hope it works out for you. And when it doesn't, ask for help. There's no shame in not being able to do it by yourself."

"My head hurts."

"Then I'll leave you to take a nap. You're allowed Tylenol. Aspirin's not recommended until your liver returns to normal size. If you're tempted, know that alcohol is not recommended on a concussion and your liver will stay swollen. It needs a break … maybe a permanent one." He turns for the door. I can't see that way because my eye is swollen shut, but I hear him gasp softly. "I warned you he needed help. He still does."

Tilly comes to where I can see her.

"How are you doing?" she asks. She looks tired, lines around her eyes I've never seen before.

"It hurts. He says I don't need pain meds, but it hurts."

"He spoke with your father about it. There's nothing I can do."

That she's still here means my dad's not blaming her for the party. There's something I've forgotten that's important, but I don't have the energy to dredge it up just yet.

"How's Cheyenne?" She looks away. My heart sinks. "I need to know."

"Shattered bones in her face and a head injury. They have her in a medically-induced coma in ICU. They'll know more in a few days."

My chest hurts so much I can scarcely whisper.

"The airbag?"

"I don't know. A lawyer is looking into it – Barnes, the one who handled the school suspension."

"Am I in a lot of trouble?"

"You were driving drunk, Peter. Of course, you're in trouble."

I wipe ineffectually at my cheek to stem the tears, but they fall anyway. Tilly gets me a tissue. I can't blow my nose because my ribs are broken. I ask for my phone and she gets it for me. I need to text Ben to let him know how sorry I am and to find out what's going on. Tilly pats me on the shoulder. She seems a little sad as she leaves.

Painful Choices

Ben

I made a decision after I got Pete's texts. I'd planned on waiting until he left the hospital and then telling him at home where the scene would be contained, but his self-serving text pushes me over the edge. I have to end this and there is no time to wait. Waiting just gives him more power to manipulate me and I've had enough of that to last a lifetime.

Before I go up to visit Pete, I stop in the ICU waiting room to check on the Theriaults. Nobody but family is allowed in to see Cheyenne but seeing them reminds me of why I have to be cruel to my best friend right now. He deserves it and maybe if I explain it the right way, he'll work on what got him in this situation.

Pete's asleep when I step into the room. His face swollen, his arm on a pillow, he's breathing shallow as if anything deeper hurts – my heart twists to see him so vulnerable. But he drove drunk and that can't be ignored, not with Cheyenne breathing through a tube downstairs.

My mind flits over Pete's million-chance history. Before boarding school, he would sometimes miss the basic cues of human society, but that was okay. The rest of his personality made up for it and he learned from his mistakes. Since boarding school – the lies, the missed appointments, the broken promises, the girls he claims not to remember having sex with, the drunken rants and the ruined outings – they all add up to just plain being fed up with him. Drunk driving is the last straw. Driving drunk and Cheyenne being in a coma – not forgivable. I should have warned Cheyenne not to get in a car with him after a party. I didn't and I feel guilty, but not as guilty as Pete should feel and doesn't.

I glance over my shoulder at the feeling of heat on my back. Alyse has floated up beside me. I indicate I'm going to the hall and she follows me.

"How is he?"

"Still pretty confused and in a lot of pain. They took him off the pain medication and he's really hurting."

"I thought he was going home today."

"His blood levels weren't quite right so they're keeping him until tomorrow." She looks tired.

"Is he sucking all the oxygen out of the room?"

"No. He's pretty quiet. I think he's shaken up and scared."

Good. Maybe I won't have to be mean for long. If he knows he's been wrong, maybe he'll show that sooner rather than later.

"Maybe you can come back and visit him when he's awake. He hasn't had any visitors but family. I think he just noticed that today. He asked for you."

"I'm not coming back to see him." She stares at me. Maybe she knows this is coming. "I'll text him." Her eyes hold a combination of dread and confusion. "Say what I have to say." I sigh. I hate this, but it has to be done. "You need to know because he's probably not going to understand and you'll need to explain it to him." She's frowning. This is a huge burden to put on a 15-year-old girl, but I can't hang around and risk Pete charming me into forgiving him.

"He drove drunk and Cheyenne may never walk or talk again." She averts her eyes and I think it's not the first time she knew he drove drunk. "I can't forgive that. I can't forgive him. He needs to stop texting me that bullshit about how sorry he is and how it was an accident. He got behind the wheel of a deadly weapon and nearly killed someone. Until he accepts responsibility for that, I don't want to talk to him."

"Don't do this, Ben." Alyse's blue eyes fill with tears. "You're his best friend."

"Not anymore. I've put up with a lot of crap from him for a long time and I'm done. If he wants the friendship, he's going to have to come my way a bit."

"Ben, he's hurt. At least let him heal before you dump this on him."

"No! I can't. I won't. He needs to change." I sigh. She wipes her cheeks. "And, Alyse. You can't rescue him either. He's dangerous when he drinks and you need to stay way away from him then, especially if he's driving. Promise me you'll do that."

Reluctantly, she nods. I've done what I can and I'm going now.

It's the hardest thing I think I'll ever do, walking away from my best friend and refusing to turn back. I sit in the lobby for a long time, trying to compose the text. I hesitate sending it and revise it a few times. But in the end, I send it because I know it's the right thing to do. Nothing has ever hurt more than ending my friendship with Pete, but maybe in time, he'll decide to make the changes necessary to salvage it.

Darkness Falls

Peter

I stare at the wall beyond the foot of the bed, my eyes gritty with salt and my chest hollow with loneliness. I know some arrangements have been made to release me from the hospital, but I don't care. Ben's not coming and that's just gutting me.

> BEN - I hate that I have to text this, but it can't wait and maybe this way you can review it later when your head's clear.
>
> Your drinking's been a problem for a long time, but I ignored it because you are my best friend and I kept hoping you'd outgrow it. And before Europe, you weren't being too stupid. You'd call a driver if you were drunk. Even that sounds

like I'm justifying your behavior. I've suspected for a while that you weren't being careful anymore – since you got back, anyway. I should have taken your keys away from you that first day at the house. Trevor told me something about you buzzing a boat in the harbor? Russell took your keys. I should have done that. Cheyenne's in a coma because you chose to drive drunk and I could have prevented that.

So, yeah, I'm responsible too, but you're not taking responsibility. Until you do, I can't be your friend. You need to stop making excuses and you need to stop drinking because I just won't put up with it ever again. I'm sorry I have to do this, but it's been a long time coming and I need to make this stand now before you talk me out of it.

I know that I screwed up. I can't go back and make it not have happened and it seems that's the only apology Ben is going to accept. I don't know what to do to change that and when I texted and asked, he threatened to block me. I can't even ask any of my other friends because nobody is responding to my texts. Well, Trevor did.

TREVOR – You need to stop, man. You're digging yourself a deeper hole. Even I'm not buying your excuses.

How is it excuses? I don't remember what happened. I only want to know what happened. After that, I stopped texting, which leaves me with nothing to do but stare at the wall and try to dig my way through an impenetrable wall with no clues to guide me.

"You planning to eat that food?"

I startle as Granddad Mike emerges on my right side. My ribs and shoulder spasm. He sees that it's hard for me to see him on that side and comes around to the left side of the bed.

"How you doing, kid?"

"Everything sucks right now."

He rubs my left shoulder.

"You definitely screwed up, but it'll get better in time."

"It won't with Ben." I hand him my phone so he can read Ben's texts.

"He has a point about the drinking, Peter. I warned you about it and you didn't listen."

"I did. I don't know how I got into that car."

"That happens when you're that drunk, Peter. Maybe if you get that under control, Ben'll stop being mad eventually."

"He'll never know. I'll be at Yale; he'll be at Dartmouth. We'll never see each other again."

"In this day of Facebook and texting, you don't have to lose touch. You just have to give him time to cool down and give yourself time to figure out what's wrong."

"Alone?"

"You're overly emotional. You'll make friends at Yale." He sighs, then looks toward the door. "It's time for you to get dressed and head home. I'm going to go out to the hall and let the nurse help you get dressed and then I'll take you home."

They gave me some muscle-relaxants a little while ago so that I can tolerate putting clothes on and moving from bed to wheelchair to car. I'm not sure how I'm getting up the stairs to my room, but I can't dredge up enough energy to care.

I wipe tears from my cheeks and Granddad Mike squeezes my shoulder again.

"You'll look back in a decade and see this as a learning experience. I know it doesn't seem like that right now, but life never stays dark forever."

Yeah, I don't see any light right now. My friendship with Ben was always the light. I just want to go home, hide in my room, and not have to think anymore. I suspect none of that is going to happen.

Letting Go

Ben

> PETER – I'm not trying to make excuses.
> Everybody keeps yelling at me about the
> accident, but I don't know how I got there. I just
> want to know how I got there.

I hand Trevor's phone back to him.

"I don't want to know, Trevor. Until he quits making excuses, there's nothing more to talk about."

Pamela plucks Trevor's phone out of his hands to read it.

"Still as manipulative as ever." She hands the phone back to Trevor. "How much alcohol does it take to blackout? Seems like someone who drinks as heavily as he does wouldn't get that drunk on half-a-bottle."

Trevor is the expert on drinking among the three of us, but I don't think he's ever blacked out. Still, he gives it good consideration before he answers.

"No, he couldn't have blacked out on a half-bottle." Trevor shrugs. "That's why I'm not buying his excuses. But he's scared and I think he cares that he's hurt her."

"Caring isn't enough, Trev. He needs to act." I'm getting kind of tired of saying that.

"Great. Does he know what action you require of him?"

"Stop drinking." Pamela glares at him. We're talking about Pete, but Pamela's now making it about Trevor.

"Yeah? That's not so easy to do when everyone's mad at you." Trevor slides off the hood of my car. "I've got to get going. I leave tonight."

"Good luck." I feel a moment of friendlessness. Trevor's been supportive since the accident – the wreck. I do it too – call it what it isn't. I need to say it clearly. Pete needs to stop calling it an accident and so do I.

"Just—think about it from his perspective. If he really doesn't remember the accident, maybe he's honestly trying to figure things out."

"I can't help him. If I talk to him, he'll work on me and soon I'll forgive him. He needs to come to me not having drank for a while and not just be upset he got caught."

Trevor sighs and indicates I should walk with him to his car.

"I hope my staying friends with him won't affect our friendship."

"No, you can make your own choices. I suggest you don't let him drive you anywhere."

Trevor giggles. He seems like he's been thinking about not just Pete the last few days. He sighs.

"So, I'm going to tell him what I know so he's not feeling quite so in the dark. He was sober when Viggo saw him in the bathroom. I think that's when he started."

Yeah, that's pretty much what I've figured out too. I've never seen Pete get that drunk so fast before, but that really doesn't matter. He was and he shouldn't have driven and Cheyenne is still in a coma.

"Just – don't block him. You can ignore him, but don't make it so he can't come back at all. Just give him some time."

Trevor's rubbing a hole in the asphalt under his shoe.

"You okay?"

"I kind of think – maybe it's my fault too. I laughed when he sprayed Hil's yacht. You know Hil's a step-brother, right?" I guess I knew that. Trevor's parents change mates yearly. "I pushed him to drink that day on the island too. He didn't want any and I kept saying it was no big deal. I didn't really listen when he said he wasn't drinking at the party. And Finn said he wouldn't give him a rematch. That's so unlike Pete."

"No, you're right. He was different that night. It was a good kind of different. But it doesn't solve the basic problem of he got behind the wheel of a car drunk and nearly killed someone."

"Yeah, I know. It's just – it could have been me. If Macaria hadn't insisted on using a designated driver as my penance for the yacht thing—it really could have been me."

"That has nothing to do with Pete. It wasn't you. It was him. Not that you maybe don't need to think about your

271

own drinking, but you did take a designated driver that night. Pete's the one who couldn't wait 10 minutes for Vic."

"Yeah, I know. I haven't had anything since that night."

"Good for you."

"I don't think I could do it if everyone was mad at me the way you are at Peter."

"I'm not changing my mind, Trevor."

He nods, sighs and opens his car door.

"See you in the funny papers, man."

"Yeah, Facebook and Insta. Have a good trip."

He drives away. I turn back toward the house and Pamela still sitting on the hood of my car. I pause, idly noticing that the "For Sale" sign to the Carson house now says "Pending." I guess the world has been moving forward in the last few days. We are all moving forward into an unknown future and I momentarily feel like I'm sliding over a waterfall and leaving my childhood behind.

What You're Worth

Peter

I need a drink. I've never felt like this before. It's a palpable thirst wrapped in an overwhelming urge for oblivion. I push myself up from the cushions and pillows and make my slow way to the dressing room and into the bathroom. All I've got is Tylenol and it's not touching the pain. I swallow two with water in hopes it'll do something. I need a drink. My skin feels like it's being sliced by a million blades of grass. I dig around in the closet shelves until I find a pint of bourbon that I don't remember stashing there. I take a sip.

My head starts pounding after the first swallow. Dr. Schaefer said a BAC of 1.8 indicated a drinking problem. And I'm not supposed to drink on a concussion. Am I crazy? Cheyenne is in a coma because of idiot behavior like this. I dump the bottle down the sink, then wish I hadn't.

It's too late now. I wobble back to bed, knowing I can't make it down to the bar.

By the time I got home yesterday afternoon, the pain had spiraled to a crescendo. I wept it hurt so bad. I finally passed out and the spasms eased. If I don't move, the pain becomes a steady entity. Propped up on cushions and pillows, I can sleep in short spurts and drowse in and out for a few hours at a time.

I'm half-asleep, the headache easing a little when a knock rouses me from my nap. A short man in his late 20s stands in the doorway.

"How you doing, Pete? Do you remember me?" He looks vaguely familiar but I can't remember his name. Can I still blame it on the concussion? "Joel Barnes. I'm your attorney." He closes the door and approaches the bed. "How's the pain?"

"Painful."

"Less painful with some whiskey, huh?"

How does he know that? I think I forgot to brush my teeth. Mr. Barnes shakes his head.

"You sober enough to have a conversation?"

"They took me off the painkillers. I was just trying to take the edge off a little." I can hear I'm justifying my behavior. Ben mentioned justifying my behavior. "It didn't work. Even one swallow gave me a headache. You going to tell my dad now?"

Barnes looks sad.

"Attorney-client privilege. Maybe you should tell him, though. Every time we meet, you've been drinking, so I'd say there's a problem and he has the means to help you with that."

I sigh, which sends a throb through my ribs. Barnes shrugs.

"I thought that's what you'd say. So, I'm here to tell you about your legal problems."

I breathe in deeply, sending a throb through my whole body.

"There was a mechanical failure with the vehicle. A steering problem. You remember that?"

"I don't remember any of it." That black hole scares me even more than the one from last spring.

"In some ways that's good because that lets the mechanical evidence speak for itself. The DA already offered to merely charge you with DUI and not push a reckless driving charge. You'll lose your license for a year, but you can get it back in nine months if you take a drunk driving education course and pay for some special insurance." I try to imagine a year without mobility, but I'm too raw from everything else right now. "Just a warning, if you're caught drinking and driving after that, your license will probably be revoked and good luck getting it back."

"I'm never going to again. I promise."

"I believe you mean that, Pete." His sadness oozes into the room. He believes me, but he doesn't.

"Do you know how Cheyenne is?"

Mr. Barnes looks even sadder now.

"That's the other reason I'm here." He draws an envelope out of his briefcase. "I get trying to call and find out how she is. You have a conscience and you hurt someone while driving drunk and you feel guilty. Perfectly understandable and I'm thinking you aren't firing on all cylinders with the concussion and pain. But they don't have sympathy. So, this is a restraining order keeping you away from her and her parents and forbidding phone contact. Okay?"

My chest tightens and my shoulder spasms. Mr. Barnes offers me a glass of water. It helps.

"Better?"

"Yeah … no! I don't know. I didn't mean for things to turn out like this"

"You know, maybe you don't want to talk to your dad about this, but there are meetings you can go to. Just find what works for you and do it."

I swallow. My nose runs. Blowing it hurts worse than almost anything. I wipe it with the tissue Mr. Barnes gives me. Mouth breathing is more tolerable than blowing my nose at this point.

"Ultimately, Pete, you're the one who needs to decide to get help for yourself. And, you're going to school, right?" I can't shrug and I can't currently imagine doing anything but lying in bed. I vaguely wonder how peeing in a fountain could have prevented me from going to Yale, but putting a girl in a coma doesn't seem to matter. "Maybe getting away from all the reasons you think you have to drink will help you not drink."

I sigh and nod. I go to Yale in a week and maybe things will be different there. Maybe I'll find a way to prove Ben wrong there or…. Right now, I'm too tired to even dream. Barnes is the only friendly face I've seen who's not family.

"Thanks for not yelling at me."

"That's not my job. I'm here to help you with the legal consequences of your behavior. But." He pauses, lays a hand on my left shoulder. "What's going on right now, Pete, will pass. But you need to address what caused it. And, I think you know that. You got away with injuries that will heal this time. Next time, you could hurt yourself a lot worse."

"There won't be--."

"Sure, you could hold yourself to a standard. Don't drink if you're driving. Don't drive if you're drinking." I think I promised myself that once. Why didn't it work? "I hope you do that – and then I also hope you'll decide to save yourself. Because, kid, if nobody's told you, you're worth not doing this to yourself anymore."

I want to believe what he's saying, but I don't. Good people don't do what I did to Cheyenne. After a few minutes, Mr. Barnes excuses himself and I return to drowsing and trying not to breathe too deeply. Maybe when the pain passes, I'll be able to think about it, but right now, it feels like I'm in a long, black tunnel with no light at either end.

Talk with Dad

Ben

> **ALYSE**–I've texted you so many times. Why are you ignoring me? You aren't mad at me too, are you?"

> **BEN**–*I'm not mad at you, Aly, but I don't want to care how Pete is doing. And that's hard because he's my best friend, but I can't care right now.*

> **ALYSE**–He got up for the first time today. He asked me to ask about Cheyenne.

I sigh. She lies for him better than he lies for himself. I tuck my phone into my back pocket and close the tailgate of the Jeep on the suitcase and action packers. I pull up at the door of my bedroom, surprised to see Dad sitting on the edge of my bed with a comic book in his lap. He glances up at me.

"Big day."

"Yeah. Feels weird."

"It's an odd time." He pats the bedspread next to him and I sit down because I know when we're about to have a conversation.

"You know we're proud of you, right?" I nod. I'm not feeling so proud of myself at the moment. "You know the Theriault girl getting hurt wasn't your fault?" I sigh.

"Not as much my fault as Pete's, but – if I'd looked harder for him, I might have prevented it."

"Well, you could have also just not gone to the party, but then a dozen kids wouldn't have had rides home and you might not have felt responsible for whatever wrecks they had."

He's making a point and I want to appreciate it, but right now, I just can't.

"He was my best friend and I've known there was a problem for a long time. I enjoyed the parties too."

"Yup." We sit in silence for a long moment. "The thing about being young is you don't know stuff. You lack life experience. You don't know what you don't know. You didn't know you were encouraging Peter and he probably didn't know what the price of his drinking would be. So, now you both do."

I wipe a tear from my cheek.

"Is this one of those things where I'm going to look back on and there'll be all these lessons?"

"Probably. Your mother and I will always support you. And, we understand why you're angry at Peter right now.

He deserves it. But I hope – in a little while when you've had some space – that you'll remember Peter doesn't have this – a dad who will sit down with him and gently explain what he did wrong."

"He's welcome to come talk to you, Dad. If I'm not here. I just can't be around him right now."

"Right. You might feel warm and fuzzy toward him before he learns the lessons he needs to learn. I get that."

"Is he calling you?"

"No. I called Tilly to see how he's doing. She says he's healing, but he's deeply depressed and she's really worried about him."

"She sucks as a parent, Dad."

"Yeah – about what you'd expect from someone her age. Thank God I didn't have teenagers when I was 25. And, thank God I didn't have damaged teenagers. Peter would have had a rough time even if his dad were home all the time. And, he isn't your fault either. That's the fault of his parents – all three of them."

"At some point, isn't he responsible for himself?"

"Yes. And, I hope he's getting that message. I hope you are too. Peter is responsible for himself. We can love someone like a brother and they're still going to do things we can't stand. That's just the way that it is. But I know you, son. Once you get angry, you stay angry. And, I hope you won't stay angry with him. If he comes to you legitimately regretful, I hope you'll unbend your spine a little and let him get some redemption."

"What makes you think that day will ever come?"

"Because I think Pete has a good heart buried under a ton of debris. But ultimately, I'm on your side, son."

I sigh and my gaze drops to the comic book. Red kryptonite. There are parallels. Clark Kent put on the class ring and became Kal who was a huge jerk. Pete drinks and – yeah. But this isn't a comic book and what Pete did to Cheyenne has long-term consequences. Then again, Clark couldn't control what he did when he was under the influence and he didn't forgive himself for what he did once he removed the ring. Can Pete do the same? I just don't know.

Dad, Mom, and Wes walk me out to the car, and we hug all around. I'm really going to miss them. Pete and I had talked about driving out together, me leaving him behind at Yale. Now I head for the ferry alone, but when I get to the Post Road, I pause and think about it. I swing over to the Shore Road. There's a van in the driveway. I don't see Pete at all. Is he in any shape to get himself packed? Maybe not. I consider texting him, but then I remember that I can't. He needs to spend this time alone, to sort it out. I put the Jeep in gear and head toward my future.

Glimmer

Peter

I'm antsy when we get there. Tilly, Vic, and Alyse help me unload my stuff since I only have the one arm. I can't lift anything heavy or make my bed. We get there early because I'm not sleeping well. I opted to go light, so it doesn't take that long to move in and pretty soon I stand outside this smack-awesome building that I wish I had the energy to care about right now. Alyse cautiously hugs me, afraid she's going to hurt me. My head's been clear for days, my shoulder throbs dully now, and my ribs still crackle when I move suddenly, but I know I'm healing. My body is healing anyway.

"You going to be okay?" she asks.

"Yeah. I don't need a driver's license here."

"You know that's not what I'm talking about."

"I'm healing."

She knows me so well and her blue eyes fill with tears of compassion.

"Call me," she insists.

"I will." She's the only one still talking to me. Of course, I'll call her.

She gets in the van and they drive away. I turn back into the building. Our early arrival meant the halls were quiet when we got here, but now people are pushing and laughing, carrying couches upstairs and I have to wait while that occurs because getting bumped right now hurts like hell. I finally make it up the stairs to the suite where my roommates and their parents are sorting out their lives. They don't need help from the one-armed drunken jerk. I turn toward my room because I don't want to talk right now.

"Peter, right?" a tall beefy guy in a New England Patriots t-shirt asks. He carries a box.

"Yeah." I grasp for the guy's name. We "talked" on email. I've seen his photo. I just hadn't imagined we'd be the same height. There are seven in this suite and though I have a private room, I share a bathroom with the guys in the adjacent room. "Rick?"

"Right. What happened to you, man?" I've seen myself in the mirror. The bruises are fading, but my eye is still a little swollen and there's a significant purple hematoma under it. And then there's my arm in the sling. Kind of hard to ignore it.

"Car accident." That explains my bruises and the reason I don't have a car. I don't have the energy to lie right now.

"What did you hit? A wall?"

"A tree." If I have to talk about it, I'm going to end up even more depressed. Besides, I'm exhausted. "I'm going in to lie down."

I should be able to nap since I barely sleep since coming home from the hospital, but I end up just staring at the ceiling for a while and finally sitting up with my back against the wall. Sometimes I imagine Cheyenne on life support like someone in a movie. Other times, I'm trying to penetrate the blank slate that is the night of the party. Alyse reports Ben is mad about the accident and advises I wait a few days. I don't know what the appropriate wait time is for trying to salvage the closest relationship you've ever had. I waited. Now feels like a transition, so I text him again.

PETER - *I'm sorry. I've been thinking about it a lot. I don't really remember the accident, but you warned me, and I didn't listen.*

I didn't close the bathroom door, so I'm not surprised when someone does. I need to be drunk to want an audience when I'm peeing.

My brain picks over all the times I could remember doing something stupid when I was drunk. Embarrassing Ben so many times. The dates I'd ruined. Insulting one of Alyse's dance mates. Getting drunker and drunker with Cheyenne that night and then nothing. I have all kinds of reasons to stop drinking, but more than anything in the world right now, I thirst for a big slug of bourbon warming my chest. What the hell is wrong with me?

My phone vibrates. Ben's reply hurts.

> **BEN- What are you sorry for, Pete? That I'm mad or that Cheyenne has to get her face reconstructed? Don't text me if you can't answer that the right way.**

Both? Can't I be sorry for both? I can't even work up the energy to be upset that he's still angry. I turn off the phone and lean my head back against the wall, closing my eyes. The bathroom door opens. I'm going to have to lock it soon as I have the energy to get off the bed. Maybe tomorrow. Rick appears in the doorway.

"You okay?" he asks. "You in pain?"

"Some. Not real bad." That first few days after Dr. Shaefer cut me off, it seemed bad, but I know it wasn't. I'm healing, now almost 10 days past the accident. I'll continue physical therapy and my shoulder will be fine. The other bruises will fade. It's everything else that's smashed beyond repair – stuff nobody else can see.

"I dislocated my shoulder once. It felt like I was dying and then it just ached and throbbed for weeks afterward. Hard to sleep."

"Yeah."

Rick's gaze wanders across my room, taking in the industrial bottle of Tylenol on the desk.

"That's all you're on for the pain?".

"Doctors took me off anything stronger after the second day."

"They're a lot more careful about painkillers these days – especially if you've ever had a problem with other substances."

I look at him for the first time. Rick's older than me by a couple of years, but in the freshman dorm. Or maybe the beard makes him seem older. Mine grows better than most guys my age, but few eighteen-year-olds could grow a beard as full as Rick's. How did he know what Dr. Schaefer said?

Rick closes the bathroom door behind him and leans on it.

"You just seem really down. You want to talk about it?"

"I can't. I don't even remember it."

"Concussion?"

"Mild one."

There's a long silence.

"Were you drinking?"

I blink at him because of the proximity to the truth terrifies me.

"What makes you think that?"

"That's usually the reason people don't remember car accidents and you were trending on social media a couple of months ago engaging in behavior that normally involves way too much beer ... er, probably ale."

I snort, which makes my shoulder throb, so I wince.

"Anyone else hurt?" Rick asks and tears prick my eyelids. I don't know this guy at all, so I blink hard to prevent them from falling, then nod slightly, swallowing the tears. "Have you talked to anyone about it?"

I remember what Dr. Schaefer said, but I didn't talk to him. What good does talking about it do?

"It helps," Rick says as if reading my mind. "It's been two years for me and, if you need someone to talk to, I'm here. And, if you want, I'm going to an NA meeting tonight at 8. You don't have to do or say anything. You can just sit and listen."

I nod. I don't know why, but it feels right. Rick breathes in deeply and lets it out slowly. We don't say anything for a minute. I've got nothing to say. I'm not admitting anything, just that I might need some help to sort things out.

"So, I know you probably dread moving right now, but there's a barbecue starting for incoming students and I'm betting you haven't eaten anything since yesterday." I don't know how he knows, but Rick has traveled this road himself.

"I don't feel like socializing right now."

"I can see that. So, your dad being your dad, I'm guessing you're not in any legal trouble."

Yeah, legal trouble. What about emotional turmoil?

"Lawyer's taking care of it. I'm going to lose my license for a year. I'm not 18, so …." I start to shrug, but my shoulder twinges a warning, so I don't. "The other person—Cheyenne—she got hurt pretty bad and that's a civil issue, but my dad says I don't need to worry about that."

"But you care that you hurt her." I nod, so wanting bourbon. "All the money in the world won't fix your guilt." My surprise must show on my face. I'd never really thought about the money. I knew some would change hands, but I didn't think it would make me feel less guilty. Now I'm really thirsty. "All the whatever-your-drink-of-choice-is won't fix it either. How many days?"

"Since the accident?" The concussion has messed with my sense of time.

"I don't care about that. Since your last drink?"

I don't know why it matters, but he's offering to help and I'm desperate to stop feeling like this, so I answer.

"Um, about a week." The need to justify myself looms. "I had some in my room when I got home from the hospital and – drinking's not recommended on a concussion. I tossed it out after my head started pounding before I even felt the booze."

Rick laughs. Is he crazy?

"Sounds like you've already done Step 1." What is he talking about? Rick reads minds. "We admitted we were powerless over alcohol … that our lives had become unmanageable."

"The second part, yeah." Rick doesn't interrupt, just slides down the door to squat on the floor. Maybe I don't need to explain, but I want to. "My life sucks and I don't see how it gets better if I'm drinking. Powerless, though. I haven't drank since I dumped the bottle."

"You want to, don't you?" Mind reading that acute has to be a superpower. Reluctantly, I nod, my mouth growing drier with every second. "And if I offered you a bottle right now, you'd take it." I start to shake my head, but I'm lying to myself and I can see Rick knows that. I nod. "That's powerless."

"Then how do you stop and stay stopped? Coz, I don't want to feel this way for the rest of my life."

"Ooo, asking the right questions. Good sign. You believe in God?"

"Not really." If this involves going to church a lot, I'm probably not going to do it. I like sleeping in on Sundays.

"You might want to revise that. You're struggling with alcoholism and God drops a guy in recovery into the room next to you. You can call it a cosmic coincidence or whatever, but I'm going to call it God. So Step 2 is recognizing that a higher power can restore you to sanity."

I feel this huge canyon opening around me so that I risk falling to my death. Somehow, Rick sees that.

"I started by going to NA and by letting people who had walked the path before me show me the way. So, let's head down to that barbecue and get you some food. I think you'll probably need a nap afterward and then we'll eat dinner and go to the meeting. And by the end of this day, you'll not have drunk. And then you can start tomorrow on another day of sobriety, but right now, today, you're just going to concentrate on what is right in front of you and not freak out about what happens a week or a year from now."

"Just today?" That sounds easy and, conversely, hard.

"Yeah. Doable, right?"

It does sound doable, so I nod, but I really want a beer right now. Maybe I could make it to the end of the day, though. I've made it to the end of seven already with no skills or guidance whatsoever.

"Is that how you get through—I mean do you still want --?"

"Yes, somedays. And when those days happen, I tell myself I promised myself sobriety for today, which tables the decision to get high until tomorrow. The first thing I do when I get up in the morning is promise myself sobriety for that day. See how that works?"

I nod. Tomorrow is always a day away.

"Of course, that promise triggers a lot of other stuff I've learned over the last two years."

"Starting with? How does that work?"

"My morning mirror talk goes something like 'Good morning, Rick. You're still an addict. Job number one today is don't do drugs.' Everything else is optional. For the first year, it needed to be, and now it just is – and I'm back in school and I think I can actually do it this time."

"So does admitting it help?"

"It didn't feel like it at first–but I was coming down off heroin, so–.But, yeah, when I looked back, I could see how admitting my life was out of control and I was helpless against my addiction meant I quit fighting the wrong enemies."

I so want to find the nearest liquor store and buy a bottle of their best bourbon and spend the night not feeling this way anymore. Rick looks right at me like he's psychic. He's kind of established that he is.

"You don't have to do it now. You could do it at the meeting or even tomorrow or the next day. But, Peter, you know."

I nod, not intending to speak, but then the words just come.

"I'm an alcoholic." A huge feeling of importance sucks the air out of the room, but other than that, I still feel like that bottle of bourbon would help me sleep tonight.

"See, the world didn't end, and you just gave yourself permission to get better."

Since we're being honest....

"It doesn't feel like it. I still really want a big ole' bottle of bourbon."

"Yeah. We'll work on that. But first, you're going to come downstairs and eat some food, because what you're

291

going through right now is way easier if you're taking care of yourself otherwise."

I still feel like crap, but maybe there is a light at the end of that deep black tunnel now. I know someone who has been there and made it back. I might too, maybe, if I try.

Step 4

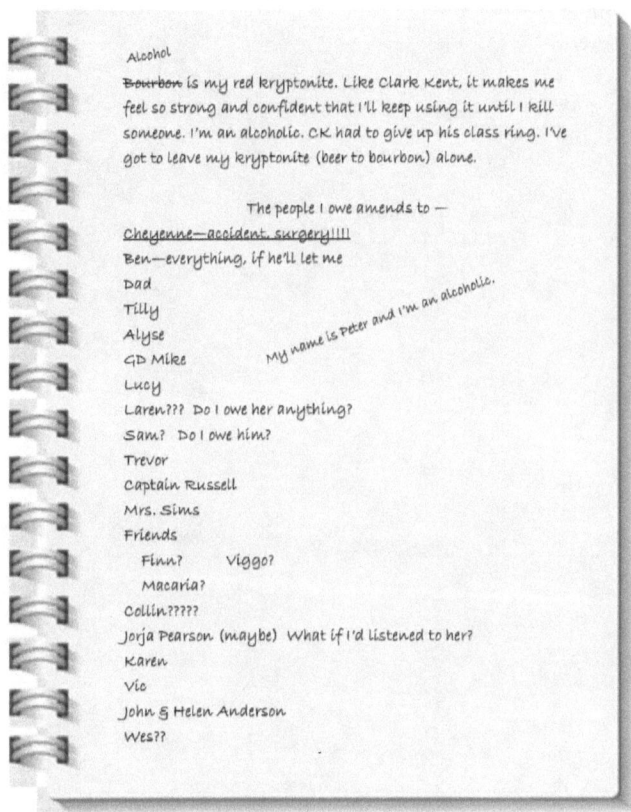

Alcohol

~~Bourbon~~ is my red kryptonite. Like Clark Kent, it makes me feel so strong and confident that I'll keep using it until I kill someone. I'm an alcoholic. CK had to give up his class ring. I've got to leave my kryptonite (beer to bourbon) alone.

The people I owe amends to —

Cheyenne—accident. surgery!!!!

Ben—everything, if he'll let me

Dad

Tilly

Alyse

GD Mike

Lucy

Laren??? Do I owe her anything?

Sam? Do I owe him?

Trevor

Captain Russell

Mrs. Sims

Friends

   Finn?   Viggo?

   Macaria?

Collin?????

Jorja Pearson (maybe) What if I'd listened to her?

Karen

Vic

John & Helen Anderson

Wes??

My name is Peter and I'm an alcoholic.

The End
###

A Word from Lela Markham

I didn't have a classic white-picket-fence upbringing. I grew up in the frontier town of Fairbanks, Alaska, and my parents were not Ward and June Cleaver. In some ways, Peter was born of the experiences of my childhood and adolescence.

But for the grace of God go I.

I came to know Jesus Christ as my Savior in high school, and—as the saying goes—embarked on a journey down a road less traveled. It took me several years to learn to allow Jesus to also be Lord of my life and in some ways, I'm still learning.

Good, better, best…never let it rest.

My husband is a recovering addict and our long-time church home had a lot of addicts in attendance. Again, Peter was born of the experiences of my young adulthood.

About a quarter-century ago, my husband's uncle introduced us to a town on Long Island, which is the pattern for Port Marion, which is not that town, but merely uses it as a real-life exemplar. Not long after we discovered the town, there was a fatal boating accident there and I wondered how the young man who was driving the boat must feel about what happened. Peter was born from that curiosity. He had to wonder "what if ...I'd done this and not that. What if...I'd stayed sober? What if...I'd listened to the adults that warned me? What if...."

What if...wasn't became the premise of a book that will come later in the series. In writing that book, I realized Peter had a whole history to tell me about—and so was born the series.

Some things to know:

Less than 1% of 12-year-olds have had a drink

About 16% of 16-year-olds have drunk alcohol

About 46% of 20-year-olds have had a drink

About 18% of 12th graders admit to getting drunk

Most teens who drink do so to get drunk.

Underage drinkers consume about 90% of their alcohol during binges (defined as five or more drinks on the same occasion at least one day in the past month, for males)

Almost 61% of underage drinkers admit to binge drinking in the past month

Teens drink and drive about 2.4 million times a month

Drinking during puberty can alter hormone levels, disrupting normal growth and personality maturation.

Drinking can lead to long-term effects on the brain, including increased risk for anxiety, depression and low self-esteem.

Teens who begin drinking before age 15 have a 41% change of developing alcohol dependency in their lifetime.

People who wait until age 21 to start drinking, have a 10% risk of alcohol dependency later in life.

Peter is a fictional character, but he's based on real-life teenagers.

A Taste of

"Walking the Centerline"

Peter

Pop quiz - Where's the one place a recovering alcoholic doesn't want to be when he's thirsty?

You guessed it in one. A blowout end-of-the-semester party in an Ivy League college dorm is probably not recommended for staying sober. It's hard to avoid when you live in the dorm. I blink through the strobing darkness at the writhing bodies, making my way toward the stairs, my nose telling me every drink I pass. I want them so-so much and yet I also know why I can't have them. People say "hi" along the way and I keep pushing. I've made it four months and I want to make it another day, so I keep pushing until I meet up with a blonde barely wearing clothes who doesn't get out of my way.

"Hey, Peter," she purrs into my ear as she drapes an arm around my neck.

"Hey." I don't know her name. She lives on the second floor. We've passed in the hall a few times.

"I want to dance with you."

"I'm still wearing my coat," I tell her. She's moving her hips to the beat of the music and I feel my anatomy rising to the occasion. Alcohol may be off the table, but safe sex is not. I nod to the stairs. "C'mon."

She giggles and we make our way up to the third floor and the suite I share with six other guys. She's already dragged me down to kiss my mouth before I get through the open and unlocked door. I can hear someone having loud sex in Lee and Jan's room – probably Jan who is headed back to Sweden for the holidays and so wants to satisfy his girlfriend before he goes. I don't even know this chick's name, but I'm hard enough to cut diamonds at the moment, so I don't care. I fumble with the lock while she tries to undress me in the common room. We fall back through the door and I kick it shut as we sprawl on my bed.

The beer on her breath is driving me crazy, screaming that I need to get some of whatever she's drinking. I don't need it, but I do want it and I almost leave her in the bed to find a cooler. She pulls me down on top of her and I forget about the cooler.

Morning dawns grey through my open window. My arm's asleep under her and it hurts to drag it free. I pad naked into the bathroom and find Jim, Rick's roommate passed out on the floor. I go back to my room to pull on sleeping shorts before nudging him with my toe. The toilet smells like a yak paddy and Jim doesn't smell much better. He groans and sits up.

"Grab a shower, man. You smell like shit." He does what he's told and I flush the toilet before using it. Rick comes to the open bathroom door.

"I couldn't find you," he reports.

"I stayed at the coffee shop until they closed and then – well --." We laugh together, but then he sobers.

"You shouldn't use sex as a substitute, man. It's just stuffing stuff down and someday, it might not be available."

"You telling me you've never done stuff to distract yourself?"

"Of course I have and still do. But you notice I distract myself with cleaning the bathroom or going for a run. I don't rely on another person to give me an endorphin boost. Girls feel good, but they don't really solve anything – especially not the way you're doing it. Do you even know her name?"

I shake my head. College has definitely changed my view of morality. I spent most of high school three sheets to the wind and moral toward girls and now I don't drink and I'm admittedly a slut.

"Enough said on that topic." Rick beckons me to his room. His side is neat, his bag packed, the bed slept in but easily smoothed. We'll be back in January. We can leave our stuff. I plan to neaten my room after the blonde left. "So, really, how are you doing?"

"Parties are hard, but I'm still sober." I'm also in the best shape I've been in since boarding school in the 10th grade. Every time I get a craving and can't find Rick or a girl to hook up with, I go to the gym. It started trying to get my shoulder back in shape after a dislocation in the fall, but it's become a way to disrupt the addiction process.

"Good. Wasn't really worried about that. You're up at 5:00 am, so …. You're headed home. You sure you're ready for that? The folks wouldn't mind a tagalong for the holidays."

"I really need to spend some time with my sister. And the way I left things in August …."

"That's Step 8. How about you work on getting through Steps 4 and 5?"

"I'll work on it. I got a little obsessed with finals."

"And, that's fine, but you need to finish your inventory – at least get enough down so you can confess it."

"You know the main thing." That one hurts.

"And we've talked about that and I feel like it's not the only thing bugging you. I mean, if you'd prefer to tell a counselor instead of me, that's fine, but you need to talk about it. You were drinking a long time before that wreck."

I nod. Jim comes into the room naked, rubbing his hair with a towel. There's no privacy in this dorm. I turn for the bathroom.

"Remember, you can call any time."

"I will. And, I already looked up meeting times. See you in January, man."

I go back to my room where the blonde is awake, looking adorable with bedhead.

"What time is it?" she asks. I look at my phone.

"Five-thirty."

"Crap!" she scrambles for the few clothes she was wearing when she got here. "My dad's going to be here in two hours and I'm nowhere near ready. Sorry."

"For?"

"You know."

"It was fun."

"I didn't pass out on you?"

"Nope."

"We did it then?"

"Yes. With a condom. You telling me you don't remember?"

She shook her head. I sigh. She clearly wanted it. She undressed me and pinned me to the bed. But it's uncomfortable to know she doesn't remember.

"Thanks for that," she tells me and then, now sort of dressed, walks out of my life. I don't know her name and I wonder if I'll ever see her again. There is something highly unsatisfying about hookups.

If you enjoyed this book, leave a review.

Watch for Book 2 sometime in 2021

Other Great
Breakwater Harbor Books

Moscow, 2138. With the world only beginning to recover from the complete societal collapse of the late 21st Century, Zoya scrapes by prepping corpses for funerals and dreams of saving enough money to have a child. When her brother forces her to bring him a mysterious package, she witnesses his murder and finds herself on the run from ruthless mobsters. Frantically trying to stay alive and save her loved ones, Zoya opens the package and discovers two unusual data cards, one that allows her to fight back against the mafia and another which may hold the key to everlasting life.

Other Lela Markham Books

Fantasy

Daermad Cycle

The Willow Branch

Mirklin Wood

Anthologies

Echoes of Liberty

Unbound

Encountering Jesus

Gateways

Fairytale Riot

Apocalyptic

Transformation Project

Life As We Knew It

Objects In View

A Threatening Fragility

Day's End

Gathering In

Satire

Hullaballoo on Main Street

Meet Lela Markham

Hi. I was raised in a house made of books in Alaska and told tales from the time I could talk. A teacher eventually made me write one of them down. I hated the exercise, but it was the spark that ignited a fire that has never gone out.

My daring husband, two fearless offspring and I live the adventure of a lifetime here on the Last Frontier where the midnight sun encourages wandering the wilderness and the long dark winters favor reading, writing and staring at the northern lights ... hence the moniker Aurorawatcher.

It's all about the aurora watching!